THE HANDS OF REVENGE

THE TALE OF THE MAGISTRATE PT. 2

JF LEE

CONTENT WARNING

Even though this is a Tao Jun story and there's lots of humor, this book deals with some sexual assault. It may be difficult to read and emotionally upsetting for some people. **If you don't want to read that stuff be sure to skip ahead to the second chapter.**

MAIN CHARACTERS

TRIBUNAL STAFF

Tao Jun

A magistrate in the river city of An'lin, Tao Jun is a talented (if not lackadaisical) investigator. His skills have earned him a high position in the local government, much to his chagrin. He's a skilled practitioner of the *Sword of the Nine Dragons* technique. In the past he was the second disciple of Master Guo, the last master of Blue Mountain.

Adjutant Ji Ping

Ji Ping is Magistrate Tao Jun's most trusted advisor and assistant. Charged with keeping the magistrate in line and on task, Ji Ping is a career bureaucrat with a photographic memory. He is usually aloof and annoyed but can always be found at the magistrate's side.

Captain Chen Yong

Captain Chen is the leader of Magistrate Tao Jun's staff. A sharp young man with a dry sense of humor, he takes his duties very seriously and is dependable.

Officer Ruo Bao

Officer Ruo is the muscle. A large and imposing man, his simple expressions hide a keen investigative mind.

OTHER CHARACTERS

Lady Tian Mei

The head of the delegation from the Luminous Moon Palace. Tian Mei is the sect's legendary Jade Beauty—a woman known for her astounding beauty.

Lady Tang Luli

The Baomu and servant of the Jade Beauty

Peng Ning

A gruff and violent man, Peng Ning is the leader of the Invisible Venom Sect.

Ding Enlai

A handsome nobleman with a lecherous side, Ding Enlai is the head of the Nineteen Panthers Sect.

———

Mao Gang

A storyteller in the employ of the Red Peony.

1

I'LL BE THE FIRST TO ADMIT IT—THIS WAS NOT MY FINEST moment. And if I were really paying attention, I would have known how this would usher in a whole rash of not-so-fine moments. What do you call a bad streak like that? A slump? A dump? A nosedive? The end of an illustrious and heroic career?

Pick one—it most likely will work.

The audience of delegates looked bored, offended, and on edge. I didn't even know you could look both bored and offended at the same time, let alone on edge. In hindsight, the joke about grandmothers catching on fire was probably not the best move. But what's the point of life if you can't have a bit of fun? Hey, their reaction is not my fault. I never knew what to say at these things, and while I could normally bluster my way through a speech, I think this time my luck ran out. I suppose that should have been a sign that things were only going to get worse.

I took three steps on the dais behind the table where a bottle of wine, a cup, and my sword, Joy, rested. Arrayed beyond that were the delegations of the Golden Chrysanthemum Summit. They had gathered at the Red

Peony, the finest inn and restaurant in the city of An'lin. Located at the heart of the Long'cheng district of the city, it was probably the most prominent establishment of the district, which meant the finest restaurant of the city and region.

And the food was better than good too.

I shifted my weight from foot to foot as I gathered my thoughts.

Three tables.

Three delegations.

Three angry and bored parties waiting impatiently for me to finish up.

There was a certain tension in the room here that was palpable, but I promise it wasn't my fault. It was already present when I got here. Maybe that's why my jokes fell flat. I'm normally a funny guy. Everyone says so[1]. But I don't really know what to say at these things. Somehow, I always managed to get sent by the governor to act as his representative.

From the name, you'd think the Golden Chrysanthemum Summit was a gathering of flower farmers, or even a meeting of the best flower wine brewers, but you'd be wrong. The summit was a meeting of the major sects in the region.

Earlier in the day, my adjutant, Ji Ping, rushed me to the Red Peony Inn for this speech. He had practically shoved me out the door of the Tribunal so that we'd make it in time. I didn't even get a chance for a snack.

"The governor wants you to welcome the delegations of the summit," he informed me as we hurried up the cobblestone streets, dodging carts of goods and pedestrians dallying about their business. "It's a really big deal."

"If it's such a big deal, why couldn't he do it himself?" I grumbled. I hated this kind of diplomatic nonsense. Look, I'm not about to be rude or anything, but smiling and grinning and telling everyone how wonderful they are was not my kind of thing.

"He has been distracted with something of late." Ji Ping shook his head. "So, it's up to you."

I scowled.

"Why couldn't he get that buffoon, Magistrate Ku? He loves this kind of crap."

"He wanted you." Ji Ping shrugged and then hurried me up the street again.

"Bah, *hundan*[2]," I complained.

I knew why he really wanted me here and it's all because of stinky laundry.

The Golden Chrysanthemum Summit *was* a big deal in the *jianghu*[3], though I hadn't been in more than a decade. It took place every two years and gathered masters from across the kingdom—though lately it only extended to those that were in the An'lin region. That exclusivity meant that really only three main sects were involved—the Nineteen Panthers Band, the Invisible Venom Sect, and the Luminous Moon Palace. A few minor clans also attended, but they were usually treated as afterthoughts and unimportant.

Years ago, when Blue Mountain was still around, Master Guo Yang, my *shifu,* would attend. As one of the senior disciples, my martial brother Li Ming and I would accompany him. The summit in those days was pretty casual. It was as much a chance for everyone to spy on each other as it was a time for old friends to catch up. There were a lot of promises of brotherhood and friendship, lots of drinking and flirting, lots of discussion about the state and affairs of the kingdom, and more drinking. It was usually a big party, and though there were some fights of honor to prove skill and settle certain points of honor, it was always a bloodless affair. Anyone who violated the terms of the peaceful summit was banned for life.

In recent years, however, there were rumors of bad blood

between the sects. Starting about eight years ago, a series of murders from an infamous serial killer named the Sickle Killer claimed the lives of prominent members of each sect. This, of course, led to a lot of finger pointing and suspicion with each thinking the others were scheming against them. While on the surface the three sects got along amicably enough, it was only a matter of time before a nasty fight emerged. I wondered why each of the sects didn't stop attending the summit, though I supposed there was more than a bit of spite there—like the need to show an ex how much better your life is without them.

So, you see? Stinky laundry.

Greeting these three delegations ahead of the summit was an opportunity to let them air out their grudges before the actual summit began. The plan was to open this meeting between the three sects, let them talk some things out, and then maybe everyone could move on and have a good time. But from the way everyone glared at each other and me, I didn't think it was working.

I suppose I should have felt honored to speak on the governor's behalf, but I hated this sort of thing. Apparently, I wasn't doing a great job at it either, judging from the cringing and wincing of Ji Ping at the back of the room.

I spread my arms wide and announced, "And without further ado, the Governor of An'lin has sent me, Magistrate Tao Jun, to welcome you distinguished guests to the Golden Chrysanthemum summit."

I waited for the applause to finish, scattered as it was.

I caught the faint gesturing of the proprietor of the establishment in the back of the dining hall, so I added, "We are also thankful for the hospitality of the Red Peony restaurant, home of the finest cuisine in An'lin. Be sure to try the Chili Crab while you're here. It's one of their best dishes, and it's absolutely divine."

The *laoban*[4] looked pleased. Beside him, Ji Ping rolled his eyes. Earlier, when Ji Ping and I had arrived at the restaurant, the *laoban* asked that I do some advertising for some of their best dishes. When I raised an eyebrow at his awkward request, he coughed and dropped a pouch of coins and then walked away. I could feel Ji Ping's disapproval from here. He doesn't approve of most things I do, and I know he especially doesn't like me taking bribes on the side. But this was harmless, wasn't it? A little bit of advertising never hurt anyone.

"The governor extends his greetings to the delegation from the Invisible Venom Sect, the Nineteen Panthers Band, and the Luminous Moon Palace. As a word of caution, the city of An'lin must remind you to be on your best behavior. Remember, you are all examples of the finest the *jianghu* had to offer," I said, trying to keep the sarcasm out of my voice. The "finest" was questionable. At best, this was a group of arrogant children with an overinflated sense of importance. "The purpose of this meeting is for you to have a civil conversation about your shared history and find a way forward from the tragedies of the past."

The Nineteen Panthers Band and the Invisible Venom Sect were kind of the run of the mill martial groups that thought they deserved a bigger piece of the action because they thought they had strong *wugong*[5]. They both took themselves way too seriously, and at times were little more than a group of organized thugs that shady people hired to do their dirty work.

At least that was the case with the Invisible Venom. The Nineteen Panthers had a little bit of a better reputation, though it wasn't exactly sterling either. Ten years ago, these two groups would have hardly been worth paying attention to, but the rivers and the lakes of the *jianghu* flow with change.

The Luminous Moon Palace, on the other hand, were a bit of a mystery. They were a proud (almost arrogant) group that had been around for decades, and if the rumors could be believed, centuries. But it was all rumor—they relished in mystery and were vague at best when answering questions about their business. On the surface, they looked like they were made up mostly of attractive women, something of a fantasy for many men in the *jianghu*. They weren't just a martial sect. They had their hands in everything. From politics to philanthropy, they were extremely well connected, and I suspected they had the governor's ear. But as far as their martial skill, that was an unknown too. I had never actually seen a member of the sect fight.

They were led today by the famous Jade Beauty, Tian Mei, a young woman of exceptional grace, good looks, and splendor. It was a title that wasn't given out easily and the young woman looked every bit worthy of it. Her face was all angles, harsh and unforgiving, but of a quality that could stop a breath with a single glance. Her gaze alternated between indifferent and deadly, though on occasion she flashed a smile to the others in her delegation that was equal parts charming and enthralling.

To my eyes, she looked uneasy and on edge to be at this meeting. She watched the other two delegations with suspicion. Rumor had it, she was a woman of exceptional martial talent as well.

"We are always on our best behavior," Peng Ning, the head of the Invisible Venom Sect, said. He was a loud and boorish man, with a wiry beard and a mane of hair that looked more at home on a patchy old lion than a human. A large man, he was the type to rely on physical intimidation to get what he wanted. "Am I right, brothers?"

A chorus of cheers erupted from their table.

"Maybe the best at drinking and being rude," Ding Enlai, of the Nineteen Panthers, scoffed. From what I remembered, he was the provisional head of the band. A handsome man, there was a certain air of cruelty and condescension about him every time he opened his mouth. Apparently, that was nothing compared to his lecherous nature. "It's not even noon yet, and you're all drunk."

A chorus of laughter from their table.

"At least we're not putting on airs like the Panthers," Peng Ning said. "It's not even noon, and they have their heads up their *pigu*[6] already."

This got a ring of laughter out of both the Venom and Luminous Moon delegations.

They then said something about the "whores" of the Luminous Moon Palace. And that got a laugh out of most of the men in the room. I don't know. I wasn't listening, but I can tell you they weren't as funny as they thought they were.

And they certainly weren't as funny as me.

"The Jade Beauty can show us all a great time," Peng Ning said.

"And if not her, then the other ladies of the Luminous Moon Palace!" someone from the Panthers yelled out.

The men roared with laughter.

A woman stood up from the Luminous Moon delegation, her face livid with anger. Dressed in pink silks, she looked to be the eldest of the group, though that did not mean she was that old. By my estimation, she was in her mid-thirties and an attractive woman—though, in comparison to the Jade Beauty, looked rather common. Snickers broke out as she rose, and judging from the snatches of comments I could hear, both delegations were familiar with her.

"Apologize to Lady Tian Mei at once!" the woman demanded.

"Why don't you let the *lady* speak for herself?"

"She doesn't need to deal with you trash, and we of the Luminous Moon will not stand for this kind of insult."

"You don't have to stand. Just lie down!"

Another chorus of laughter.

"Please, if I could have your attention for a few more

moments," I said, trying to head off the impending argument. I may as well have swapped my *futou*[7] for an opera mask and started singing for all the attention they were giving me. Peng Ning and Ding Enlai glared at each other, and Tian Mei, the head of the Luminous Moon delegation, and the woman who spoke, glared at them both.

I sighed, realizing how difficult this task the governor set before me had become. *And if things go wrong, he can blame me instead of taking the fall himself.* I made a mental note to myself to find some way to get back at him.

I raised my cup, toasting everyone that was assembled here today. It took a couple of moments for the grumbling and glaring to stop, but I waited patiently until they had raised their own cups.

"To your good fortune and good behavior," I said, draining my cup and holding it out to them. "Or face imperial wrath," I murmured to myself.

They drained their cups, and I made to get off the dais when the Jade Beauty spoke out. "The Governor of An'lin has nothing to fear from the Luminous Moon. It's the Invisible Venom and the Nineteen Panthers that should watch themselves."

"Is that a threat?" Ding Enlai asked. "Are you going to send the Sickle Killer after our brothers again?"

"We had nothing to do with that," Tian Mei said with a sniff.

I frowned. It seemed like the Sickle Killer still haunted the city. Apprehending him was one of my first successes in An'lin. It should have been old news but apparently was still a point of contention between these groups.

"Lies! I know how you Luminous Moon types are. If you're not going to send a glorified assassin, then you might just send yourself. You, Tian Mei, caused the fight last time! You broke Wu Bei, our former leader." Ding Enlai hissed.

"And it was the boorish behavior of Peng Ning that brought a disastrous close to the summit!"

"Why would we hire an assassin to kill your people? The Sickle Killer murdered our own as well. Even an idiot can tell that makes no sense," Tian Mei snapped. "Though I suppose a piece of logic like that is too much for your limited intelligence."

Peng Ning cackled. "Aww, is poor Ding Enlai afraid of the Sickle Killer? Don't worry, we'll protect you."

"What are you implying?" Ding Enlai sneered.

"I don't have to imply anything."

I bit back a curse. It really didn't take much for them to be at each other's throats.

"The Sickle Killer is dead!" I shouted over the din. "It has been eight years since he stalked your ranks and still you fight amongst yourselves. You're all here early at the governor's invite to settle your past grudges before the rest of the summit delegations arrive. Can't you please unite in the tragic memory of your fallen comrades and move on?"

"Yes, listen to Magistrate Tao Jun—the Hero of An'lin[8]," Ding Enlai said, nodding at me. "After all, our illustrious Magistrate brought justice to us all by catching the Sickle Murderer."

Hero? I fought the urge to scowl. "Maybe you can settle your differences in a way without so many insults?"

"We'll settle our differences! Clear the floor. Let's fight, Ding Enlai, Tian Mei." Peng Ning shouted as he rose. He jabbed an accusatory finger at the other two tables. "You've sullied our names long enough."

"Hmph," Tian Mei said. "You don't need us to sully your names. You do that yourself."

"We have a claim against the Luminous Moon as well!" Ding Enlai from the Nineteen Panthers shouted as he stood as well. "In fact, our claim supersedes yours!"

"You dare?"

"Obviously we dare! The so-called Jade Beauty hurt our former leader after she was betrothed to him! By right, she is ours. She owes us her blood!"

"Convenient of you to bring up such a claim, Ding Enlai," Tian Mei sneered. "Especially when you benefited the most from his injury."

Ding Enlai scowled and slammed a hand on his table.

"The Jade Beauty assaulted me as well!" Peng Ning retorted. "I have a claim on restoring my honor."

"Maybe if you weren't so ugly, then you wouldn't have a problem!" Someone said, and laughter erupted.

The older woman in pink silks stood up from the Luminous Moon delegation, looking to shout something at the other two tables, but the Jade Beauty rested a hand on her arm. "It's okay, *Baomu*. I'll handle it."

"You can't," the older woman shook her head.

"I'll handle it."

"Awww, does the little Jade Beauty need the permission of her *baomu* in order to fight us?" Peng Ning mocked. His table roared with more crude laughter.

"These men think they own you," the older woman said bitterly.

"Then I'll show them how mistaken they really are."

"Oh, she's going to show us," Ding Enlai said. "There's something else you could show us as well!"

Rude laughter.

I rolled my eyes. What were these people, adolescents? Still, childish or not, the tension in the room was palpable. I bit back a curse. I was almost out of here and now a brawl was going to break out on my watch. Ji Ping wasn't much of a fighter, the other guards that followed in our wake were incredibly outclassed by the martial talent assembled here today. They'd be unable to do much in a fight.

Well, everyone except for me, of course.

I don't know how to break it gently, so I'll just come out

and say it. I'm pretty good with a sword. I mean, I would have to be. After all, I am a disciple of Master Guo Yang of Blue Mountain. And I am the second last swordsman to practice the Sword of the Nine Dragons *jianfa*[9].

I shifted my weight again, my eyes darting to my white sword perched on the table in front of me. Close enough to snatch if there was trouble, but I was hoping it wouldn't come to that. Any time there's blood, there's trouble.

And paperwork.

I hate paperwork.

And I was on a sort of probation anyway. When the governor gave me this assignment, he warned me in no uncertain terms that I needed to be so extremely careful. Not only were things delicate between the three sects, but apparently, after the last three cases I solved ended with someone losing a limb, getting wrist tendons slashed, or put in a coma, I needed to tone down the violence.

Of course, I tried to explain to the governor that at least I got results, but he was in one of those moods and wasn't having any of it.

Maybe I should just let them fight and get it out of their system.

"Please, please, let's have none of this," I said half-heartedly, but no one was listening. To be fair, I didn't care if they fought. If they wanted to punch each other senseless, who was I to intervene?[10]

The delegates began moving the tables, pushing them back to clear an area in front of the dais to fight. The *laoban*, a balding middle-aged man dressed in the livery of the Red Peony, sprinted across the room to my side. Following close behind was a young man I didn't recognize. The youth grinned at me, but the *laoban* looked grim.

"Are you really going to let this happen, Magistrate?"

"Humph, why not?" I shrugged. "If they fight and can get over it, we'll have a peaceful summit and everyone can go home happy."

"Oh, but my restaurant," he wailed. "The damages alone will cost a fortune!"

I frowned. He reminded me of Yan Tao from the Broken Furniture Inn[11]. Proprietors are always so touchy about things like broken furniture and damage to their establishments. I mean, sure, they have a point. But how else are people supposed to settle their grudges? By going outside and fighting?

Preposterous.

"It'll be okay," said a young man at the Laban's side. "I'm sure Magistrate Tao Jun will come up with a solution that would be equitable for all." He looked barely out of his teens, and I would have guessed that he was part of the waitstaff, but he wasn't dressed in the uniform of the Red Peony. Instead, he spoke to the *laoban* in a manner that indicated more than a passing familiarity.

Not a son, I thought. *Who is this kid?*

"But…" the *laoban* started.

"Let me make an announcement," I said, placing a reassuring hand on his shoulder. "I'll take care of you."

He looked uncertain but gave me a single nod. "Thank you, Magistrate."

By now, they had finished pushing the chairs and tables back, clearing enough of a space that was wide enough for a fight. Tian Mei, the young woman known as the Jade Beauty, strode forward. Long sleeves, elegant. She looked more like a princess than a fighter of the *wulin*. She looked up at the dais and gave a thin smile. At first I thought she was smiling at me, but I quickly realized she was smiling at the young man who had come up with the *laoban*. The young man, for his part, gripped the edge of a chair tightly, his knuckles turning white with worry.

Interesting.

Across from her stood Ding Enlai, who winked at the young woman and received a glare in return. Peng Ning, the bearded leader of the Invisible Venom, flexed and stretched. The men of his delegation cheered.

A three-way fight. This will be messy.

"Before we begin, I must have some reassurances. If you break any of the furniture or the restaurant, you must promise to reimburse the owner of the Red Peony. I expect cost plus forty percent," I said, gesturing at the *laoban*.

There was a murmur of disapproval from the group.

"Fifty percent then," I said with a shrug.

Silence.

"You can fight, just behave."

"That will be acceptable, Magistrate."

"Any cost will be worth it to get some payback."

"Hmph," the Jade Beauty snorted.

"Further rules—once this fight is over, there will be no reprisals. Understood?" I fixed each of the delegations with as deadly serious a glare as I could muster. "The winner of this fight will not be dragged into any more discussions about the Sickle Killer or any other incidents from the past. It will be considered dealt with and done."

The two men cupped their fists and bowed to me.

Jade Beauty gave a single nod, without taking her eyes off of the others.

The older woman at Tian Mei's side looked worried, and she said something to the Jade Beauty. The Jade Beauty reacted angrily, but I couldn't hear what she said.

Ding Enlai, Peng Ning, and Tian Mei settled into fighting stances.

"Begin," I said.

They circled each other.

"How about an extra wager?" Peng Ning said.

"What's that?" Ding Enlai said.

"The winner of this fight gets to show the Jade Beauty a good time."

"Ha! You're on. But I have another idea," Peng Ning said,

waving his opponent close. He whispered something in his ear that no one else could hear. When he was done, both men were grinning like idiots.

Her eyes narrowed.

Whatever sympathy I may have held for the two men evaporated as I felt my lips curl in a scowl. Even when a woman was strong enough to break their faces in half, men like Peng Ning and Ding Enlai would deride them as though they were less than human. Typical behavior for many men in the *jianghu*—I didn't approve.

I hope she shows them how good a time a broken face can be.

"A really good time," one said. The other guffawed. Their minions chuckled too, though they didn't know what the joke was.

There was no way this was going to end well. In hindsight, I should have called the fight there, but I was curious as to what these three delegates from the top clans had to offer.

Peng Ning launched his attack first, a leaping punch attack that would have caught the Jade Beauty in the chest if not for her quick turn away from the main force of the blow. Peng Ning then twisted and kicked out towards Ding Enlai, who caught the strike with his palm.

For her part, Jade Beauty avoided the more straightforward linear strikes of her two opponents. She was a spin of action, a dodge of agility and grace. From watching her fight, I knew that she was holding back.

What are you waiting for?

Ding Enlai of the Panther adopted a modified Tiger-style *quanfa*[12]. He curled his palm back in a tiger palm and struck out with slashes and strikes. Each fighter struck and blocked, dodged and countered. A three-way fight always turns into a sort of dance—a feint, an opening, and a counterattack. No one was ever really safe in the middle of a three-way fight.

There were no allies; only opportunities that could turn on you in a single moment.

And yet...

At some unspoken signal between Peng Ning and Ding Enlai, they both simultaneously attacked the Jade Beauty. But it wasn't an ordinary attack. Ding Enlai moved to cut off her evasion and grabbed her from behind. Peng Ning grabbed at her chest, snagging her robe, and tugged down.

A loud rip.

Tian Mei yelped and struggled to grab her ruined robe to cover her undergarments. Her face turned bright red as she tried to turn away from the hands brushing across her body, and she scrambled back a few steps. The tables from the Invisible Venom and the Nineteen Panthers roared with laughter. Understandably, the Luminous Moon delegates shouted in anger.

Was this what they had planned together? I frowned. I wanted to look away to protect the young woman's modesty, but with the fight still going on, I couldn't. *They never had any intention of fighting fair.* I felt a flare of anger, but kept it in check. I wondered if I should intervene, but this chaos was what I had allowed to unfold, and I wanted to see where it would lead.

"Oh, whoops. That was an *accident,*" Peng Ning said, snickering.

"Peng Ning! Have you no honor?" the older woman shouted as she hurried to the Jade Beauty's side. "How dare you touch her!"

"Oh, it was a joke, lighten up," Peng Ning said. "We're just having some fun."

"I didn't expect someone called the Jade Beauty to be so flat!" Ding Enlai quipped. His companions laughed.

"If she didn't want a good time like this, she shouldn't have dressed that way!" Peng Ning yelled to more cheers.

"Let me go," Tian Mei hissed, shrugging the older

woman's hands from off her shoulders. She tied her robe so that it wouldn't droop, then straightened. "I can handle this!"

"Although, if the Jade Beauty liked what she felt, I can arrange a more personal encounter," Ding Enlai said. His delegation guffawed.

"Oh, but I can show her a good time too," Peng Ning. "She might enjoy my touch a little better."

Without another word, Tian Mei leaped forward and grabbed Peng Ning by the hem of his robe.

"Oh, she wants more!" Peng Ning said, eying her hand on his robe. He grinned. "Not here, sweetheart—I'll get out of my robe somewhere a little more private."

He really should take this more seriously, I thought. "Can't they tell she's holding back?"

"What do you mean?" the young man who accompanied the *laoban* asked. Startled, I glanced at him. I was so focused on the fight that I didn't realize that he was still on the dais with me.

"It'll take too long to explain. Just watch," I shrugged.

And then everything happened all at once.

With one hand clutching the hem of Peng Ning's robe, Tian Mei used her free hand to slap him across his face in a short, quick strike. First, Peng Ning laughed, but his amusement quickly turned as she unleashed a whole sequence of slaps. Palm after palm struck him in the face, before a final punch to the chest sent him flying into the crowd. His minions, as loyal as ever, dodged out of the way and he struck a table, shattering it in the process.

A thin smile lengthened across my face as a grim sense of satisfaction filled me.

"My table!" the *laoban* cried. He must have seen my smile as he pouted severely, as if to chastise me. "That was dark oak. Very rare. Very expensive."

"They'll pay you for your damages, *laoban*. Don't worry," I soothed.

The crowd went quiet, and with a sniff, the Jade Beauty straightened her robe and turned to leave. The rest of the delegation moved to follow, but the older woman turned and glared at Ding Enlai and Peng Ning.

"You'll pay for the way you humiliated her," she said, her voice quivering with anger.

"No reprisals," I warned. "Peng Ning ripped her robe, and Tian Mei taught him a lesson."

"But, Magistrate!" she protested. "They dishonored us."

"You all agreed to the terms of the fight," I snapped a glare at the woman. A moan came from the table Peng Min crashed into, and the man stumbled to his feet. "Besides, I think Tian Mei has taught her lesson quite effectively."

"It's not enough," she said. "Scum like this don't understand."

I glared at Ding Enlai and Peng Ning. "And what you did is completely unacceptable."

"Oh, Magistrate, it was just a good joke."

"It wasn't funny," I said. "And I'm a man with a great sense of humor. Apologize now."

"Apologize to who? The Luminous Moon have already left," Ding Enlai of the Panthers laughed. "That idiot never stood a chance. Peng Ning is a loser who deserved to be beaten."

"What did you say? You dare insult us like this?" someone shouted, and the room turned into a din of yelling and shouting as the remaining Venom and Panthers faced off with each other. Peng Ning struggled to his feet, shrugging off the help of his companions. Ding Enlai smirked at him and beckoned him to fight him again.

"What are you going to do about it? Send the Sickle Killer again? We know it was you!"

Time to intervene.

"Enough!" I shouted, and in a single motion, I lifted Joy with a flourish and unsheathed it. With a quick downward slash, I cut through the table in front of me. Ji Ping yelped, and the *laoban* moaned.

The sudden thump of the breaking table caught their attention, and I leaped in between Ding Enlai and Peng Ning.

"This is over, agreed?" I pointed the tip of my blade towards the two factions, making it as clear as I could that I would not tolerate further fighting.

They nodded.

"Then this matter is resolved. If I hear any of you speak of Sickle Killers again or blame anyone for anything, you will spend the rest of the summit in a cozy cell at the Tribunal," I warned as I sheathed my weapon. "Enjoy your stay."

"Yes, Magistrate," Peng Ning reluctantly growled.

"As you wish," Ding Enlai said with a note of mocking. I glared at him, and he feigned innocence.

As their delegations made their way back to their rooms, the *laoban* tugged on my sleeve. "Excellency, the table!"

I shrugged. "Send the bill to them."

2

A DIFFERENT SORT OF AMBUSH AWAITED ME WHEN I GOT HOME that evening.

"You want me to what?" My mouth hung open. In a life full of handsome and fine moments, I'm sure it wasn't one of my finest, most handsome moments.

"I want you to get married again," she said.

I stared at my wife, Shao Lan. I could feel the skin at the back of my neck crawling with agitation, my eyebrows furrowing as I tried to understand her latest insanity. "You want me to what?"

"Get married," Shao Lan repeated, this time with an irritated edge in her voice.

"In case you haven't noticed," I said, crossing my arms, "I'm already married."

"Obviously," she snapped with more than her fair share of annoyance. "But you need to get married again. I talked to your mother about this."

"Oh, good," I said dryly. "My mother." No good could ever come out of my wife and mother conspiring together.

"Yes, your mother. You should listen to her more often."

"I listen to her as often as I listen to you," I said. Which, to be fair, was not that often. Maybe she didn't know that.

She glared at me.

I guess she knew that.

"I'm lonely here," she said with a sigh. "You don't understand."

"What do you mean, you're lonely? What do you call all these people that answer your every whim?" I said, waving my arms towards the paper paneled door screens. It was highly likely that the servants were eavesdropping. Sure, they would never admit to it, but that's what they do, right? We boss them around and then they complain about us and gossip about us behind our backs.

Wasn't that the natural order of things?

"Those aren't friends," she said testily.

I sighed. *Friends.* She wants friends. I tried hard not to roll my eyes. Everyone wants friends. Do we get them? More often than not, no, we don't. Friends are for the young, and when we get older we go through our lives sad and lonely and unwanted and then we die. End of story.

The natural order of things.

"Then what about all the salons and everything you go to? Don't you get together with the other official's wives and...do whatever it is you do?"

"That's not the same," she shook her head. "I want someone to keep me company here," she said, jutting her chin forward in that adamant glare I knew so well.

I was clearly in trouble.

And there was no way I was going to win this—not with Mother involved.

"Thus, the only solution," she proclaimed with a smile, "is for you to get married again."

I couldn't believe that I once thought her smile was charming. Ours was an arranged marriage—my father arranged some kind of deal with another minister in the capital, and blah blah blah, next thing I knew, I was supposed to marry his daughter. I braced myself for the worst, but I was surprised at our wedding that she was pleasant to look at. I'll admit, I was nervous, and then she smiled at me with that little charming smile, and I thought to myself, *wow, I must be the luckiest guy ever.*

That was then.

Who knew luck could be so finicky? It didn't take long for me to learn that smile meant she wanted something, and that nothing would stand in her path to get it. The first few requests I happily obliged, because I, like a complete *bendan*[1] had no defense against it. Jumping ahead a few years and now I can't even come home to my own house anymore. It's not my house. It's hers. I just live there.

And now she was securing her place on the throne.

May all the gods in the celestial bureaucracy[2] *please save me.*

"I have to get married again so that you'll be happy?"

"I thought you'd be excited by the prospect of another wife. Most men are."

"Since when have I behaved like most men?"

She scoffed. I think I should have been offended.

Another woman here would be a headache. It was bad enough that Shao Lan behaved as empress of the house—all under the roof answered to her terrible fury. Another woman? That would be disastrous. Catastrophic. Calamitous. Cataclysmic. Fatal.

I could see the well-wishers and mourners at my funeral already. "How did he die?"

"He married a second wife."

"Oh, that would do it."

And then they would laugh and talk about something else. I hoped they at least thought to make an offering of hell money in the brazier. Maybe a palace or two. I was worth that at least, right?

Maybe.

"I don't have time to look for another wife," I said gruffly, hoping that this ploy would at least buy me some time.

"I know. That's why your mother and I already did the work."

Oh no.

She smiled at me. This one was no innocent and sweet smile. It was a wicked and triumphant smile[3]. She knew she won.

I was an idiot. I should have seen this trap coming.

Assassins? I can handle that.

Soldiers? I can handle that.

Bandits? Pffft. Not even a problem.

But this woman?

Somehow, she's always able to conceal her plans so well. If she had the interest she could have toppled Lady Yue for control of the underbelly of An'lin and ruled over the entire city. Luckily for all of us, she wasn't. Instead, I'm ambushed by my own wife. I'd just finished a hard day of solving crimes and sending bad guys to prison, and then suddenly, BAM. I'm dead.

Death by wife. Write it up on the autopsy report.

Most criminals would sell their own fathers for an ambush like that.

"We picked out three women that would be acceptable to us. All you have to do is pick one."

Did I have a choice in the matter?

"Who are these unfortunate women?" I grimaced, expecting the worst.

"Hmph, I'll have you know they're refined ladies of the highest pedigree."

I sighed. That was code for pretty, but idiotic. I glanced at her, and I didn't know her wicked smile could grow even more wicked. "So, who are they?"

"I sent three scrolls to your office."

"You what?!" I all but yelled.

"I thought since you never spend any time here, you'd want to examine the scrolls at the Tribunal." She said this in such a nonchalant, innocent way that I knew she did it on purpose.

I groaned. Knowing my men, they wouldn't be able to keep their nose out of it.

She ruined me. It was all over. I was doomed. I may as well move to the capital at Chang'ping and start all over again. My men would never be able to look at me with respect again[4].

Maybe a big case would come up and that would buy me some time before this inevitable and tragic fate that awaited me.

I was never that lucky.

3

As if my earlier conversation with my wife wasn't bad enough, things only got worse at the Tribunal office. The next day, I entered my chambers on the west side of the building. When I entered, I found my staff huddled around my desk, deep in speculation.

It's never a good sign when your people are hanging around your desk and you're not there. Was it an official summons? Maybe another reprimand from the governor, a formal written censure? Our last conversation hadn't gone well. Immediately after my speech at the summit, he wanted a report. I told him my version of it.

"It was fine," I said, trying to play it off nonchalantly. Maybe he hadn't heard what happened. I wasn't going to bring up the fight, and I certainly wasn't going to bring up what happened to the Jade Beauty.

"Fine?" the governor said.

"Fine," I repeated.

"Fine?" he asked again.

"Fine," I said.

"*Goupi.*[1] It wasn't fine!" He slammed a hand on his desk.

"I told you not to let a fight break out, and you encouraged one!"

I guess he heard what happened.

"Things were already tense enough from the Sickle Killer murders years ago, and then the Jade Beauty assaulting Wu Bei of the Panthers last year, and now this? If you weren't so good at your job, I'd have you flogged."

He was always threatening to flog me but we both knew that I was his best. Magistrate Ku, for all of his posturing, wasn't even a close second.

That was earlier this morning. After an earful, and a lot of shouting and apologies, I made my way to my office, where I found my staff around my desk, gossiping about something juicy. They liked to do that. Apparently, I need to work them harder.

"I didn't know the boss was such a pervert," Captain Chen said in a loud whisper. "I've never known him to visit the pleasure houses."

Captain Chen was more or less my right hand at the Tribunal. A sharp young man with a face that was all angles, I trusted him to keep our department running and the officers and staff in line. Maybe as a result of that, he had creases on his face that marked the permanent frown he always wore. He was a career man, and you couldn't ask for a better person to keep things going when I wasn't around. I'd never tell him that, of course. He'd be going places if I ever let him out of my staff.

"You would never have guessed," Ji Ping said, shaking his head in disappointment—again. Let's face it, I'd never be able to please Ji Ping. He was always disappointed in me. He didn't have any family, so he was basically married to his career. As my adjutant, he was the one I worked most directly with. A short kind of guy with a round face, he was the definition of by the book. He kept an immaculate appearance, thoroughly enjoying keeping his officer's uniform as tidy and in order as you possibly could. He typically wore a *futou* to cover his baldness. That level of attention to detail carried over to the job. He knew my schedules and, more often than not, did my paperwork and kept me on task. If I was being honest, I'd say that I couldn't do my job without him.

I'm never honest. I'm a liar, and I know it.

But I'm a damn cool liar.

"Just when you think you know someone," Captain Chen mused.

"I guess you really don't know anyone," Ji Ping sighed.

To be honest, I was surprised at Ji Ping and Captain Chen getting along. On any given day, they had a healthy dislike for each other. But, somehow, that rivalry enabled them to work really well together. Everyone knew it even if they would never admit it.

Unless, it seemed, when it came to ganging up on me.

"Guess he's just like the rest of us," Officer Ruo said. Ruo had a slow way of speaking that matched his massive size. To say he was a big man was an understatement. But behind that muscular form and deceptively slow manner of speech hid a great investigator with a good nose for clues.

"Hmph," Ji Ping said.

"Hmph," Captain Chen agreed.

I have such a hard life.

"Are you going through my mail?" I asked, interrupting their speculation. They jumped, backing away hurriedly from my desk. I folded my arms, frowning at them with my best attempt at a withering glare. Usually, I have a good glare. I learned it from my mother, who learned it from her mother, who learned it from her mother. I'm not sure how I picked it up instead of my sister, but that's probably because she's an idiot. But my glare only had half the power that my mother's and grandmother's glare did. Maybe it's because I'm not a woman. Or maybe it's because it only works on people that respect you.

And my staff were not really a group you'd say respected me, at least not convincingly. But today it worked, and they scattered under my glare. Captain Chen and Officer Ruo hurried to their desks. Ji Ping straightened but lingered near my chair.

"Well?" I snapped, waiting for an answer. They squirmed. I glanced down at the scrolls on my desk. Sure enough, like the wife had promised, three scrolls, each with a painting of a different beautiful woman.

"No, it uhm…" Captain Chen stammered.

"Well, you see…" Ji Ping started.

"There was a fragrance to it. And that was kind of suspicious," Ruo said.

"And then a gust of wind blew open the windows…"

"And the scroll fell on the ground…"

"And unrolled," Officer Ruo finished. "We had to see what it was."

It was a good thing they were officers of the law and not criminals. They looked guilty beyond guilty. If guilt had a personification, it would look like these three buffoons. They were, without a doubt, the worst liars I'd ever met[2].

"Well, they're very beautiful women, Magistrate."

They snickered amongst themselves.

"Oh, and Tian Mei, the Jade Beauty," Officer Ruo swooned. He pointed at the scroll on the top of the pile. "She's wonderful."

"What is this? I thought you were in love with Bai Jingyi[3]?" I growled.

"Oh, I am. But this is something altogether different," Ruo responded.

"They said that if you make eye contact with her, you fall completely under her spell. No man can resist her," Captain Chen explained.

"I saw her palanquin arrive for the summit. I was on my

patrol and the curtain parted and we locked eyes," Officer Ruo sighed. "She's incredible."

I frowned at Officer Ruo's swooning. I'd known him to be the first to fall madly in love with a woman—there were times where it felt like there was a new one every week. But this? This was a full-on intoxication.

I was beyond startled. The Jade Beauty, the woman that destroyed Peng Ning yesterday, had an arrogance to match her strength. This is the kind of woman my wife wants to add to the household? Disaster didn't even begin to describe how bad this was. I was beyond doomed. Maybe I could move to the far north, over the walls of the northern capital, and live among the nomad tribes. I could pledge my service to the commander of the northern armies, She Who Pacifies the North. That would be a better fate.

"She's dangerous," I said, remembering the way she sent Peng Ning flying.

That could be me.

"Who cares? With that kind of danger, you could die a happy man," Officer Ruo swooned.

"Would that I could be so lucky," Captain Chen sighed.

"You'd be a better catch if you stopped frowning all the time," Ji Ping said.

"What do you know?" Captain Chen snapped.

"I know, because I am a good catch."

"Good for catching mice, maybe!"

"What do you know about mice, you rat-faced idiot?!"

I take back what I said about Captain Chen and Ji Ping getting along. I let the two of them bicker. A bit of discord in the office keeps things interesting and their skills sharp.

They were well into their fifth round of barbs when the sliding door slammed open and a pale and bewildered clerk burst into the room. He nearly fell over as he stumbled through the open doorway. He recovered his footing, then nearly fell over again as he hurried to me. "Magistrate! Magistrate Tao Jun!"

"Unless you're looking for someone else, that's me," I said dryly.

"Magistrate! Thank goodness you're here," the clerk gasped.

"What's going on?" Captain Chen and Ji Ping said at the same time. They glared at each other.

They could be so cute sometimes.

"Magistrate, murder!" the clerk said.

I frowned. "Are you telling me that I should murder someone?"

"No, no, no! That's not it."

"Watch your tone," Captain Chen snapped. "You're speaking to the magistrate."

"Show some respect," Ji Ping sniffed.

Maybe they did respect me, I thought with a bit of pride.

"Apologies, Magistrate Tao Jun," the clerk said, cupping his fist and bowing deeply. "Please forgive this one."

"Sure, sure," I said dismissively. "But you better start talking, or I'll have you cleaning the latrines for a month."

His eyes widened. He didn't know that I wasn't really going to make him do that, but I'm not going to lie—there's something quite entertaining about making the clerks squirm. It's probably because they make my life complicated. They were always clamoring for my attention or having me sign something. Clerks were responsible for processing much of the paperwork that kept a city like An'lin running as efficiently as it does. They collect the proper documentation and send it to the various officials for stamping their seals. You might call it doing their job, but I call it making my life difficult.

And I don't like people that make my life difficult.[4]

The clerk opened and closed his mouth a few times like a fish gasping for air as he struggled to find the right words.

"Come on, spit it out," I encouraged, slamming my fist on the table. Sometimes a show of violence encourages people to start talking.

"There's been a murder!" the clerk squeaked.

"Oh, is that all?" I said, a little disappointed. "That happens all the time. Contact Magistrate Ku. He can help you with that."

"But Magistrate Ku sent me over here to enlist your help."

I groaned inwardly. That damn Ku *would* try to pawn off this problem on me. He and I had something of a gentleman's feud. He didn't like my position close to the governor and the concessions that the governor gave me, and I thought he was a stuffy moron that should be demoted to be a clerk.

Actually, that's too good of a position for him.

Maybe he should be a wooden chair.

Naw, a wooden chair had more charisma than he did.

"Fine, what's so special about this murder that I need to look into it?"

"Uhm…" the clerk looked around the room, his gaze darting between each of my staff before meeting my gaze. He looked like he was going to throw up. "It's because…"

"Come on, hurry up," Ji Ping said. "The magistrate is busy with important matters. Don't waste his time."

"If you're quite done, you can leave," Captain Chen said.

"I insist," Officer Ruo said, as he straightened to his full height.

There are these completely unsubstantiated rumors around the Tribunal that my squad and I are the most difficult team to work with. I don't know where anyone gets that stupid idea.

"The victim was Peng Ning of the Invisible Venom Sect! Someone killed him at the Red Peony!" the clerk all but shouted. "Dismembered!"

Stunned silence. I nearly fell out of my chair in surprise. Peng Ning was no slouch. Sure, he got his butt handed to him by the Jade Beauty, but he was a real paranoid bastard. The last time I met him outside of the summit, Peng Ning had just defeated a group of bandits that were raiding a village close to An'lin. By the time the An'lin guard could be dispatched, he had single-handedly trashed all the bandits. He stood outside of the gates of the village grinning like a madman as we arrived.

"Dismembered, you said?" I asked.

The clerk nodded as he turned green.

"*Hunzhang*[5]," muttered Captain Chen.

Hunzhang indeed.

"You saw it yourself?" I asked the clerk.

He nodded. "It was gruesome."

I looked from the face of the clerk turning paler and paler to the scrolls of alluring and demure women that my wife wanted me to choose from and I felt a twinge of existential dread. Attractive yes, but they were another set of chains I wasn't too keen on wearing.

A murder on the other hand...

"All three of you better come with me. I'll need an extra set of eyes[6]," I said, barking orders. "Go get your weapons. Hurry up!" They scrambled. Ji Ping retrieved an extra pad of paper and his favorite brush for writing. Officer Ruo and Captain Chen strapped on their swords.

"We've got a murder on our hands," I said with a grin.

The clerk ran out ahead of us, and I thought I heard him vomit out in the hall.

4

I'VE ALREADY TALKED ABOUT HOW THE RED PEONY IN THE Long'cheng district was one of the most exclusive inns in the city of An'lin. It's typically frequented by the wealthy of the city and the surrounding regions; it was known as a place of opulent decor and decadent food.

But what I didn't say was that it was a restaurant of the ultimate discretion. There was an unspoken law that governed the place—what happened within the walls of the Red Peony stayed secret. How they managed to do that when the nobles of An'lin liked to gossip must be a secret as precious as their chili crab recipe. That's what made it the perfect place to hold the Golden Chrysanthemum Summit.

A vicious murder tends to disrupt that kind of wariness.

I never ate there much—too ostentatious for my tastes[1]. A huge three floor restaurant, the outer facade of the building was only topped by its luxurious interior. Guarding the front entrance were two enormous stone lions, sculptures that were nearly as tall as Officer Ruo. Rows of red lanterns hung from the eaves of each floor and even this early in the day, there was a buzz of activity around it. There was usually a long line of hopefuls waiting outside of the restaurant, those that weren't fortunate enough to get a reservation but still dumb enough to try to get in. The reservation system was a barrier to entry of sorts. If you had the right connections, you didn't need a reservation. You simply had to show up.

The crowd today, however, were not hopefuls, but rather curious onlookers.

"Make way!" Officer Ruo bellowed as he cleared a path for us. "Make way!"

Seeing the massive form of Officer Ruo shoving his way through the crowd, the smart ones hurriedly got out of the way. The dumb ones were shoved hastily to the side. There are a few reasons why I keep Officer Ruo as part of my staff. This was one of them. Most people find him intimidating—which is why I keep him around. I would like to say that he's a gentle giant and that his size matches the largeness of his kindness and his heart, but I'd be lying.

And we already know that I'm a liar.

"First one to throw up buys the rest of us lunch," I said to my squad as we walked up the stairs towards the Red Peony. "What do you think, boys?"

"I'm not paying for anything," Officer Ruo said, glowering at the city guards keeping the onlookers from entering the restaurant. The wide-eyed guards backed away from Officer Ruo, stunned at his size.

"Then don't throw up," Captain Chen growled.

"I'm not going to throw up," Officer Ruo insisted.

"Says the man that threw up the last three times," Ji Ping said.

"It was the smell last time!" Officer Ruo protested.

"I hate to say this, but shall we focus on the task at hand?" I asked, eying the horrified look the other guards were giving us. Sure, it's bad humor to make light of a crime scene, but when you've seen as many dead bodies as we have, you have to make light of it a little bit or else the whole prospect will drag you down.

When we entered, we found a pair of guards trying to console the trembling *laoban* of the place. Ji Ping moved to join them and to collect his testimony of what had happened. Captain Chen exchanged a few words with another guard and then lead us to the private bedroom suite where the murder happened.

The interior of the room could have belonged to any of the wealthiest of An'lin—Lady Yue, Lord Chen Hutong, or Master Shun Li. Dark hard wood paneling adorned the walls of the room. Elegantly etched scroll work on the lattice screens. Wooden peonies carved into the chairs, the table, and even the sliding door panels.

That was where the elegance ended.

The brutality began with the partially dismembered corpse docketing the center of the room. I shook my head, frowning at the sight in front of me. Peng Ning was propped up on a chair leaning against the table, and his hands had been removed at the forearms. His throat had been slit, but I couldn't tell if that had been the fatal blow. There were large cuts across his abdomen as well, and his entrails hung from the chair.

I gagged.

Keep it together. You don't want to buy everyone lunch.

And then there was the message written in blood on the wall's paneling: "You'll never touch anyone ever again." That wasn't ominous at all.

Captain Chen and Officer Ruo began their inspection of the room in opposite corners of the room, and I thought I saw Ruo convulse like he was going to throw up. But seeing me grinning at him, he recovered and pretended like nothing happened.

Grisly.

There was a lot of violence here, and clearly someone had a grudge against Peng Ning—you don't go to the lengths of cutting up a body unless you *really* didn't like someone. As I scanned the scene, I could feel something clicking away in my head like the abacus of an apothecary merchant.

What is it? I thought, trying to place my growing unease. There was something oddly familiar here, and I couldn't quite place it.

"Two other victims over here," Captain Chen reported, looking grimmer than usual. He prodded at a corpse with the scabbard of his jian. "Still kind of fresh."

"A third over here," Officer Ruo called out. "Lots of blood."

"Almost too much blood."

"How much blood can a person have?"

"Well, it's not all one person here. It's kind of mingling."

"Ew."

"I'm just calling what I see."

"You could say it with more tact," Ji Ping scolded.

"But it's all over the walls and on the artwork too!" Captain Chen said.

"And that creepy message."

"That too!"

I let them argue. The truth was, their bickering not only kept each other sharp, but it also kept me sharp too. I scanned the scene, and I could feel my frown pulling my face downwards. There was something about this scene that felt familiar, but I wasn't seeing it yet. The Red Peony wasn't some back alley in He'bian. The Long'cheng district was as upscale as you could get outside of the imperial capital. A popular hangout of the nobles of An'lin, everything in the district was catered to the wealthy.

And I mean *wealthy*.

Things were likely to get more complicated. If the nobles were spooked, they'd say something to the governor. And if enough of them said something to him, then I'd be on the hook to do...something. Anything. Sometimes that just means making a show of doing a lot of things, like forming a task force and going on a few patrols that locked down the neighborhood in a show of force.

But a murder like this, I'd probably have to *actually* do something.

Like solve a crime.

Officer Ruo was right. There was a lot of blood here. I stepped gingerly around the crime scene, being careful to not let my robes touch any of the blood. Look, laugh all you want, but it's really hard to get blood out of silk. Not that I know from firsthand experience, but the servants often complain about it loudly enough that it's a problem.

I looked over the corpses of the two men that were not dismembered. The first two victims appeared incidental—an afterthought. They were muscular men of the kind of build you'd expect from goon bodyguards. Judging from the insignia on the hem of their robes, they belonged to the same sect as Peng Ning. I thought I recognized them from the day before, but I could have easily been mistaken.

On both bodies were deep gashes across their throats that stretched from ear to ear. *A curved blade?* I'd have to get the coroner to check the depth of the cut later. Their hands bloody from their desperate attempt to stem the flow of blood. Their clothes stained red from the chest down. One fatal wound each. Their killer didn't care who they were—they were just in the way.

Which led to Peng Ning's corpse. I felt my frown go deeper. *You were always a mean bastard. Who did you piss off this time?* The answer, of course, was everyone. He wasn't that likable, and after yesterday, it was easy to guess who would have had it out for him.

Ji Ping coughed politely at my side, pinching his nose to block out the stench. From the way his face wrinkled, it was clear that it wasn't working.

"Not a good start to the summit, eh?" I said.

"I don't think it was the start the governor wanted when you let them fight," Ji Ping said, shaking his head.

"You think this is probably related to yesterday."

"That's up to you to figure out, Excellency. I just record the facts," he said with a shrug.

"Do you remember how badly Peng Ning was hurt?"

"He took quite the hit from Tian Mei, but I believe he would have still been in fighting condition," he said with a sniff. Ji Ping had a low opinion of *jianghu* types. He thought they were little more than criminals. And there were definitely times when he was right. There were a lot of mercenaries with no morals that were willing to fight for anyone willing to pay them.

But Peng Ning was no ordinary low ranking pugilist of the *wulin*. He was a prominent leader of a major sect in the province. He may have acted like a maniac, and had a coarse manner about him, but he was still not an easy target.

So was this the Jade Beauty then? Yesterday, I had silently cheered her on as she fought Peng Ning and felt some satisfaction when she sent him flying. But now? *She would be the obvious choice.*

"With the summit in town, it's going to be busy around here. You three start talking to the patrons and the staff of the place—especially those that are involved with the Summit." I gestured at the other guards. "I don't want anyone leaving the Red Peony without my approval."

Keep them all trapped. Maybe someone will make a mistake.

As long as that's not me.

"Yes, Magistrate," Ji Ping hurried away.

"Whoever our killer was, they had time to set this up. This wasn't just a murder. It was clearly a message," I mused.

"What's the message?" Officer Ruo asked from across the room.

"You mean other than the one written in *blood?*" Captain Chen yelled back.

Officer Ruo gagged.

"That's what we need to figure out," I said. I felt my unease grow. I stared at the body again, the grotesque way it sagged in the chair. I could feel that I was staring right at the question, the answer, the mystery, but it all eluded me. I pounded my fist against my leg in frustration.

Peng Ning wouldn't have gone down without a fight. I took a deep breath, held it for a moment, then let it go. I closed my eyes. Here's something that I'm good at that no one else knows—sometimes, when I focus, I can see the unseen. I don't mean seeing things like *gui*[2] hiding in the shadows. But if I focus hard enough, I can sometimes see the expulsion of qi. Sure, it doesn't sound that impressive. I know that most masters of the *wulin* can see the flow of qi in a technique. It's high level stuff, but pretty ordinary.

Where I'm different is that I can see how every exertion of qi leaves behind a mark on the environment. It's almost like following ink strokes on a canvas. For a few hours after the fact, I can make out the trace of qi.

I took a deep breath, fought the upcoming gag reflex, and then opened my eyes, scanning the scene again. There weren't any signs of a fight or a struggle. None of the furniture was smashed. I closed my eyes to confirm it and there were no afterglows, no resonance that would give us some insight to the fight.

Nothing.

What happened? I wondered again, stroking my beard.

I added up the facts again. Deep single stroke cuts across the neck on the bodyguards. Peng Ning with his hands removed and set on grisly display. No sign of a struggle—the significant martial skill of Peng Ning rendered useless.

Oh no.

It finally made sense. I had seen this kind of crime scene before. I felt my blood go cold.

It's not possible.

Look, I don't know what anyone else will say, but I can say for certain there's a definite scale to bad days. On one end, you have mild inconveniences—maybe you dropped your book on the ground and now it's mudstained. Then you have annoyances— the fish ball vendor didn't provide enough curry for dipping. Then you have disasters—I've already talked about the ambush my wife laid out for me today, so I'm not going to get into that anymore. And then there are catastrophes—maybe the house burns down. Maybe someone important and close to you died.

And then there are outright calamities. Seeing the way the limbs were splayed out around the room, the mess of blood and entrails, would normally be a disaster. Hell, this kind of murder is usually a catastrophe. But seeing as this was a murder I thought I had solved ten years ago?

That's something else.

"Looks kind of familiar, doesn't it?" someone said from behind me. I didn't know the voice.

"What?" I asked, turning to see who spoke. It was the young man from yesterday—the *laoban's* young friend. The kid had a lazy kind of look about him. He carried a *pipa*[3] that he slung over his back. He wore the same tunic as yesterday, plain but elegant. He looked wide-eyed at the crime scene but didn't seem disgusted by it. That, I thought, was odd. I fixed him with a look of suspicion. "Who are you? And who let you in here?"

"Forgive me, Magistrate Tao Jun. My name is Mao Gang," he said, cupping his fist and bowing. "I didn't get a chance to introduce myself yesterday with all that was going on. I'm a storyteller that has taken up residence in the Red Peony."

"A storyteller, huh?" my eyes narrowed. I looked for the guards that were supposed to be keeping people from entering the scene, but they were nowhere to be found. "You're not supposed to be here."

"It's the Sickle Killer, isn't it?"

I must have made some kind of idiotic face because the storyteller started grinning sheepishly at me. Another not-so-fine moment. I scowled. "What makes you say that?"

"Well, your reaction, for one."

"Maybe I'm just surprised at how gruesome this crime scene is."

"The Sickle Killer was one of your first cases in An'lin," he stated. "He murdered so many people during his time here—all of which were members of the Invisible Venom, Nineteen Panthers, and Luminous Moon. And this scene...it's just like the stories: Hands cut off. Collateral damage caused by deep slashes to the neck with a curved weapon. You brought in the murderer and the Tribunal executed him. It brought you a lot of acclaim!"

"You remember that? You couldn't have been more than a kid." I had to hand it to him. He knew his stuff. If it really was the Sickle Killer, then this was a ghost of the past—a literal one.

It can't be. I watched him die.

"I was a kid," Mao Gang said. "But you couldn't go anywhere without someone talking about it." He paused for a moment and took on an almost shy expression. "When I heard those stories as a kid, I was absolutely enthralled. You are my hero, you know? Magistrate Tao Jun, the Hero of An'lin!" he moved his arms in a dramatic flourish. "I've followed your career closely and all of your successes." He bowed again to me. "I'm so glad I finally got to meet you."

I frowned again. *Hero?* I didn't know anything about that, but I sensed a con. There are no heroes worth following—not in this era. And the thought of me being someone's hero? I don't know how deluded someone could get, but this was a whole new low.[4] He didn't notice my frown and kept going.

"And, this is kind of embarrassing, but…I use your cases in my stories. *The Tales of the Magistrate* is what I call them."

"You what?" I asked, dumbfounded for the second time in as many seconds.

"I tell your stories. Oh, those are some of my best tales— the crowd loves them[5]. They also love the stories about your sworn brother, the Last Swordsman of Blue Mountain."

"He's not the 'Last Swordsman of Blue Mountain,'" I growled. "In case you've forgotten as well, I trained there too, and I'm not dead yet![6]"

"What's going on here?" Captain Chen said as he approached with Ji Ping. He frowned, fixing Mao Gang with a suspicious glare. "Who is this?"

I didn't bother to explain, but the storyteller bowed to them and introduced himself again. "I was just saying to the magistrate that this crime scene looks like the Sickle Killer."

"The Sickle Killer?" Ji Ping repeated, startled.

The already grim-faced Captain Chen frowned even harder.

"There's no way," Ji Ping said. "He's dead. He can't hurt anyone anymore."

The storyteller shrugged.

"There's no way it's the Sickle Killer," Ji Ping insisted. "I watched him die."

It was true, Ji Ping was there too. He had more hair back then and was Magistrate Bao's adjutant, but I remembered how grim he looked then.

"It's true," Captain Chen agreed. "I watched his head roll."

I didn't remember Captain Chen being there, though he may have been a guard on duty at the time.

Ji Ping nodded his thanks to Captain Chen.

"Check the inside of his mouth. See if there are flower petals in there," the storyteller said. "If it's the Sickle Killer, there should be chrysanthemum petals."

I felt a shiver run down my spine. That was a detail the general public didn't know. How did this kid find that out?

"Boss?"

"Check it."

Captain Chen gingerly stepped over to the corpse of Peng Ning and pried opened the man's mouth, reaching a finger inside. Sure enough, he extracted three chrysanthemum flower petals. We stood around in silence for a few moments, each contemplating the petals in Captain Chen's fingers.

"Boss?" Captain Chen asked quietly, waiting for me to answer. "Could it really be the Sickle Killer?"

"I don't know." I sighed. "Whatever it is, we've got a real problem on our hands," I muttered.

In the corner, Officer Ruo heaved and vomited.

"Lunch is on Ruo!" I exclaimed.

5

PENG NING WAS PARTICULARLY PROBLEMATIC, EVEN THOUGH HE was the victim here. He had a reputation of being willing to do anything for a good paycheck. He was a tough bastard, known for being a little on the lecherous side, and was perfectly willing to knife someone to get what he wanted. In hindsight, I don't know why we didn't arrest him earlier.

Well, sometimes things have a way of sorting themselves out.

With a victim like Peng Ning that made enemies everywhere, it meant that there were a lot of potential suspects, and a lot of people to interview. There are two kinds of interviews I usually conduct. The first was the more 'pleasant' kind. I politely request a conversation, and we might sit around a table, usually in a private office at the Tribunal, and we'd chat. Sometimes I'd pour tea. I'd review the statements collected by the guards and my staff and try to find inconsistencies.

It's true what they say about investigative work. It's a lot of monotony with a few moments of excitement. A lot of it is looking at little things, looking for little details that no one would notice—the skew of a hat, the way a leaf crunched underfoot, the depth of a footprint. Each minor detail is another brushstroke on the canvas of the case, and in the end, answers, justice, and maybe someone loses their head.

At least that's what is supposed to happen. In reality you talk to people—a lot of people— and you look for alibis, mistakes, and contradictions. You find the tension and the pain points and you dig your fingers into the open wounds and sometimes, if you're lucky, they squeal enough to tell the truth.

The second kind of interrogation was the 'unpleasant' kind—though there were times it was amazingly satisfying. Instead of requesting a conversation, I'd demand it, and that meant armed guards busting down doors and dragging people kicking and screaming to the Tribunal. That kind of conversation involved a bamboo cane, whipping, tears, and a lot of screaming. Other than the violence, it was similar to the first kind of interrogation. I was still looking for inconsistencies in their story, only this time I prodded at literal pain points and wounds, in the hopes that they would squeal enough to tell the truth.

Some magistrates, like that idiot Magistrate Ku, jump right into the second kind of interrogation. They think it brings them the fastest results, and yes, they are right. A person under enough pain would scream anything to make it stop. When the Sickle Murders first struck An'lin, that was the type of solution I opted for. I left a trail of screams almost as bad as the body count of the murderer. It was the biggest case I had ever gotten, and I wanted to close it as swiftly as possible. It's a problematic solution, though. You never know if it's the right answer—or if it was simply an answer.

For some magistrates, an answer was enough.

But I'm not like most magistrates.

This time around, however, I knew I couldn't be sloppy. I needed responses and testimonials I could actually work with. It wasn't a case of just finding someone to punish—I needed to find the right person to punish. We also couldn't let things get big and out of hand or the nobles would get spooked at having murders in their district. Their pain meant more headaches for me.

My staff confined everyone to the Red Peony and began their interviews, only calling me in for the finishing touches on key individuals. Whatever else I may say about them, and I say a lot, I do trust them to do their jobs. They're good at vetting the right people for me to talk to in a case.

At the inn, they narrowed that down to ten people. As I sat down in a quiet backroom of the Peony, I ran through the usual gamut of questions:

"Did Peng Ning have any enemies?"

"Did he do anything suspicious during the days leading up to his murder?"

"Did he eat anything different?"

And we got the usual gamut of answers in return:

"We all have enemies."

"Nothing more suspicious than usual."

"Soup dumplings." That last one made sense—no one goes to the Red Peony without getting soup dumplings. They're absolutely to die for.

Well, not literally.

The answer to the first question was also true. You don't make it far in the *jianghu* without making a few enemies—especially if you're a part of a martial sect like the Invisible Venom. Seeing as the first Sickle Killer's murders were all revenge killings, the obvious move was to find out who *really* had it in for Peng Ning.

As it turned out, everyone had something against him:

"That bastard owed me money."

"That jerk made a pass at my wife! I would skin him alive if I had the chance."

"Good riddance he's dead! He's such a creep."

Even his own people of the Invisible Venom Sect didn't like him:

"The man was an utter slob."

"He'd pick fights with people and then leave us to deal with it."

That made me sad for the rest of the day. No one liked him at all. One day, if and when I die, I hope someone says something half nice about me. Maybe something like "Oh, he had some good jokes," or "Wow he was such a great hero. I wish I could be like him," or even "Let's build a giant statue of him and put it outside of the Tribunal."

Yeah, that last one.

The restaurant staff was very accommodating. They answered whatever we needed to the best of their ability, and I believed them. They had overlapping alibis and appeared genuinely distraught by what happened on their premises. After I finished conversing with them, they brought us food and refreshments, and I may or may not have had a few soup dumplings during my interrogations.

I mean, come on, we're human right? The Red Peony's perfect *xiao longbao*[1] is a marriage of land and sea. It features the natural sweetness of the local crab and the fatty deliciousness of pork wrapped together in a beautifully delicate skin that's just waiting to burst in your mouth.

Damn, I need another order of them.

The guards ransacked each of the delegation member's rooms searching for clues. I don't know how effective this process really is. They rarely know what to look for, but it serves its purpose of setting people off balance. And that unbalance was worth its weight in gold ingot.

Out of the ten people we interrogated, there were really only three that I wanted to talk to. But the members of the sects weren't nearly as cooperative or helpful. From the thin answers they gave us, they didn't have very good alibis—especially not Ding Enlai and Tian Mei.

The delegations were spooked. The possibility that a murderer, even a dead one, could stalk and kill someone of Peng Ning's martial caliber was a scary thought. The sects kept to themselves and regarded everyone with hostile suspicion. They disrespected my people, which meant that I had to go in and bully them into giving me better answers. I don't get it. If they were only helpful when we first talked to them, then we wouldn't have to go through this whole song and dance where I make *everyone's* lives miserable.

There was a lot of shouting, banging on tables, smashing chairs, before they'd even give me second-rate answers.

There are a lot of tears involved[2].

Everyone had something to hide.

Ding Enlai, the head of the delegation from the Nineteen Panthers sect, sat across from me, smirking. He was a young man in his mid-twenties, noble born, and fairly well connected. He bore the smug sense of self-assurance that comes from someone that had everything given to him in life. He came to our meeting smelling faintly of wine and was dressed in green silks embroidered with cats. I thought it was a little on the nose, wearing a robe of cats when he belonged to a Panther sect, but there's no accounting for style. Not everyone can be as handsome as me.

His fashion sense didn't stop him from smirking at me, though. I knew him personally—we weren't close or anything, but I thought he'd be more cooperative. Instead, what I got was his full jerk persona. I knew the type: the smirk was all false bravado. He was terrified, and it showed in the little details. His hands were cold and pale, the blood draining out of them from stress. He kept turning his head as though he could catch someone sneaking up behind him.

Before I could start, he stated, "You hid it well, Magistrate

Tao Jun. I hear you're going to marry Tian Mei, the Jade Beauty of the Luminous Moon Palace."

"Is that so?" my eyes narrowed. *That wife.* She must have already been spreading the news to force me into making a decision about this. I'll admit, his statement definitely threw me off guard for a moment. But I'm used to this sort of thing, so instead I shrugged it off. I suddenly saw an angle and let him tug at the thread.

"Everyone is talking about it," he said.

"Is that so? Nothing has been finalized yet," I said dismissively.

"Good, I might still have a chance," he chuckled. "It's not every day you hear that one of the most powerful families in the kingdom is getting married to one of the most beautiful women in the kingdom. You're a lucky man. She's a beauty to die for," he said with a lecherous grin. "The things I'd do to a woman like that..." he mimed some rude gestures.

I didn't know the Jade Beauty that well, but at that moment I wanted to slap him across the face and out through the gates of *diyu*[3].

Idiot.

"You better watch out! Pu Er of the Gate sect and Yin Qiao of the Wheel are both obsessed with her as well. You know what we should do? We should get together—maybe we can all have some fun with her," he cackled.

I slammed my hand on the table between us, cracking it. Ding Enlai's eyes went wide at the sudden sound. "Right, well, we're here to talk about death," I said instead. "And a Sickle Killer returned from the dead."

That caused him to blanch, but he kept grinning at me.

"Is it really the Sickle Killer?"

"You tell me."

"You're the magistrate that arrested him. Tell me something," he said, leaning in close. "I heard, you know..."

"What?"

"He uses his sickle."

"Obviously."

"But he uses it to...you know?"

"Out with it," I said, getting annoyed.

"He removes things," he said, and for a moment, the bravado cracked and a hint of nervousness entered his voice.

"You mean you're worried the Sickle Killer will use his weapon to remove your manhood." It was my turn to smirk. I curled my finger and made a slicing gesture.

He winced.

"Tell me about Peng Ning's death. You saw him the night before."

"Yeah, I heard about that. Tragic stuff," he said nonchalantly. He thought he had the advantage here, now that I let my temper show. If there's one thing you should know about me, it's that half of it is a show.

The other half is a lie.[4]

"Bullshit, tragic. You had it out for him—everyone knows this. In fact—" I jabbed a finger at him, "I witnessed a very, very public disagreement yesterday between you two."

"Hold on..." he said surprised. "You don't think that I..."

"You killed him," I sneered. "Given your collective history, you staged the murder to make it look like the Sickle Killer to put fear into the other delegations. You snuck into Peng Ning's room, killed his men, then killed him. It's a simple enough case. You're completely guilty. All that's left is to see you beheaded."

Sometimes you just have to hit them with the wildest accusation and really sell it by shouting in their face. Against a man full of smarmy bluster, it was a trap that worked surprisingly well. And if you did it right, out of sheer shock, they'll admit to the crime. Case closed.

"Now hold on, I had nothing to do with that," Ding Enlai protested.

Damn. Guess it didn't work today.

"You can talk to me now, or you can come down to the Tribunal and we can have our conversation there. Or do I need to remind you about our dear friend, Eight-Fingered Wu?"

"Eight-fingered Wu?" He stiffened and started shifting nervously in his seat. The sense of ease and confidence he carried had disappeared.

"Did you forget who made him 'Eight-fingered?' You may as well confess. You killed Peng Ning. If you confess now, then we'll only behead you. If you don't, then we'll torture you *and then* behead you."

"I didn't! Peng Ning and I were friends…"

"Lies. Everyone knows that Peng Ning didn't have any friends. He screwed you over and you wanted to make him pay," I jabbed an accusing finger at him again. "You waited until the Jade Beauty took a piece out of him, then snuck into his room and killed him!"

"That's not true! Okay, yes, everyone knows about the Waterfall incident. But it's not like that, I swear. We got over it, and now we have a few laughs about it."

"The Waterfall incident? I know for a fact that you've killed men for less than that." I didn't, but he didn't know that.

"That's not it!"

"And you're just getting some payback for it by killing Peng Ning!"

"I'm innocent in this!" He cried again. That was a lie. Everyone that says that is guilty of something. I guess we all are in one way or another. "I wasn't with him when he died. I was with…"

"Who were you with?"

"Well, one of the serving girls from the Red Peony—"

"And she helped you murder Peng Ning?"

"No!"

I leaned back in my chair and gave him a hard look. He

struck me as being on the edge of tears. His bravado had melted away. I fought the urge to roll my eyes. A coward, yes, but a coward whose idiotic bravery would return to cover his insecurities soon enough.

"The executioner has a new axe—a gift from the governor. I think he's looking to test it out. It really doesn't matter who he tries it on."

"Okay, okay, maybe I was exaggerating a little bit and we didn't get along that well. But I didn't have anything against him. We sometimes do jobs together. But I swear, we're drinking buddies now! Sure, we have some public arguments, but we even chase a few of the same girls together—like the Jade Beauty. Wow."

I gave him a look that told him exactly what I thought of his explanation. He kept bringing up the Jade Beauty. Apparently, she was something of a fixation.

"But I would never kill him!" he quickly added. "I swear on the Jade Beauty."

"You're kind of obsessed with her, aren't you? You keep bringing her up."

"Only because she's the most desirable woman in An'lin. I mean, everyone has made a pass at her. Even Peng Ning, last night. I wanted to see that fool crash, so I steered clear of her, and wow, what a crash."

"You mean he made another pass at her last night, after he was already beaten by her?"

"They have some very good liquor here. Maybe it made him too brave," Ding Enlai said. "But since he's gone, and you don't seem to want her, she's going to be mine. She just doesn't know it yet." He smirked. I didn't like that his bravado was returning. I needed to put an end to it.

"He's dead, and you're going to go after her now? That's not helping your case." I sneered, leaning over the table. This fixation with the Jade Beauty was worth looking into, but first I needed more information. It was a good thing she was on the docket to have a conversation with. "In fact, it's making you look more guilty."

"That's not what I meant!" he stammered.

"You killed him so you could get to the Jade Beauty. That sounds very probable to me," I said. And for some magistrates, that would be enough. Slap on a solution to a problem—no matter how weak—and call it good.

"I didn't do it," he said quietly. "You have to believe me."

"I don't."

"It was someone else." His eyes widened, and his voice took on an almost desperate pleading. "I know who it is—it was Tian Mei, the Jade Beauty. She wanted revenge, see? She was humiliated, and so she murdered him."

"Stick around," I said. "I'm going to have more questions for you later. You're not to leave the Red Peony."

He was an idiot—that much was clear.

"But…"

"I don't care."

6

"EXCELLENCY, WE HAVE A PROBLEM," CAPTAIN CHEN SAID AS I exited the room.

"What's wrong?" I nodded for him to follow. As we walked, I glanced over my shoulder at Ding Enlai. His dour expression warmed my wicked heart.

"Members of the Invisible Venom delegation are trying to leave. They started harassing the staff of the Red Peony and are trying to get past our guards."

"So? Make sure they stick around," I ordered.

"Well, we are, but they're making a lot of noise. The *laoban* is getting worried and wanted you to come and deal with it."

I let out an exasperated sigh. As if I didn't already have enough going on with a possible reappearance of a dead murderer. "Where are they now?"

"By the main entrance, Excellency. Shall I take you there?"

"Please."

We worked our way through the backroom hallways of the Red Peony, emerging onto the second floor of the central dining area. From the top of the stairs, I could see a quartet of guards standing with their swords drawn across from a group of ten men all wearing the uniforms of the Invisible

Venom. They barred the exit to the restaurant and looked nervous as the delegation grew angrier. A group of men and women in the serving attire of the Red Peony watched in concern. From the looks of their group, it looked like the delegation may have roughed them up a bit. Ji Ping watched the group with growing consternation and seemed relieved when he saw us descending.

"You can't keep us here!"

"We're the victims. You can't do this to us!"

Officer Ruo stepped between the two groups. The delegation lost a bit of its bravery and rancor as they eyed his size. Even if his martial skill wasn't anything special, his girth certainly made up for it.

"I'm sorry, but this is Magistrate Tao Jun's orders. No one is to leave the Red Peony until our investigation is complete."

"But we're—"

"I said, 'No one is to leave the Red Peony.'" I approached Ruo's side. I made sure that both groups saw my sword clutched in my hand. "What's the meaning of this?"

Officer Ruo gave me a grateful nod and stepped to the side.

"You can't keep us here, Magistrate! We're not prisoners."

"Is that what this is about?" I snorted. "You're whining because you think you're prisoners? Would a prisoner have access to such delicious food?" I gestured towards the Red Peony staff. I wondered if I could get another plate of dumplings after this.

"We have rights! You can't keep us here!" A man with thinning hair combed over the top of his scalp jabbed a finger in my direction. He sneered at me, and I caught a foul whiff of his breath. *Rotting teeth—no wonder he's so upset.*

I laughed, which had the odd effect of silencing the group.

"Ji Ping, tell this group what kind of rights murder suspects have," I said in a deadly tone.

"We're innocent! He's the head of our sect!" Thinning Hair protested.

Ji Ping cleared his throat, trying his best not to sound nervous in front of the group. I have to give him credit. He prefers to stay in the background, but he did a pretty good job. "If they are under active investigation, they are required to comply with everything we need."

"And since you're all under investigation," I said, pacing between my guards and the delegation, "you have no rights. For all I know, you killed him yourself, and then tried to blame it on someone else."

"You can't do this!"

"This token gives me the authority to do this," I snatched up the magistrate seal at my belt, showing it to all in the room. I stared every one of them in the eyes, glaring at them with all the fury I could muster—which, given the circumstances, was quite a bit. "You should be grateful that I don't just take you all into the Tribunal for a more *exhaustive* conversation. We have tools there that are very…persuasive."

Most of the group glanced at each other nervously.

"But seeing as some of you are in such a hurry to leave, maybe you're hiding something from us. That wouldn't be the case, would it?" I threatened.

A few of them shook their heads. They were the smart ones. Unfortunately for me, the loud ones are never the smart ones.

"It's obvious that it was the Jade Beauty!" Thinning Hair said. "She has had it out for Peng Ning for a long time! You should be arresting her!"

"It's not Lady Tian Mei," a voice said from the edge of the crowd.

The storyteller.

"And how would you know?" Thinning Hair hissed. "Are you her personal—"

"That's enough," I said, cutting him off. This man was

getting on my already short nerves. "Return to your rooms and stay there."

"We don't have to do that," Thinning Hair said. "Come on, boys, let's get out of here!"

Thinking he had the support of his fellow delegates, he tried to push me out of the way and make for the door.

That was his mistake.

Maybe I let my emotions get the best of me. Maybe I was a bit rattled by the possibility of dealing with a ghost from my past. Or maybe I was just looking for a fight—that happens from time to time[1]. It was another not-so-fine moment, and I knew it.

But I didn't care.

The guards are trained in crowd control, so I could have left them to deal with him. Maybe a quick shove and he'd fall over backwards and then they'd detain him. Maybe they'd get in a nice, casual beating and then go on their way.

Instead, I decided I wanted to make an example of him. As his hands came to push me aside, I turned to the side, and striking out with the pommel of my sword, hit him full in the face.

"Ahhhhh!" Thinning Hair cried out. His hands rushed to his face, and he fell to his knees. Blood gushed from his mouth, and he spat out a couple of teeth as he moaned.

Joy's white blade sang out as I unsheathed it. I held the blade aloft in a flourish.

"I am Magistrate Tao Jun—The Magistrate of the Torch. I have burned villages for less than the idiocy of this filth." I nodded at the moaning man. "If anyone else has any objections, I would love to hear it."

No one spoke.

"Now, I suggest you return to your rooms and stay there. The Red Peony staff will be happy to take your orders— provided you are polite and pay well. If I catch word that any of you are bullying them, we can arrange more *comfortable* quarters at the Tribunal." I made sure to look each member of the delegation in the eye. At least some of them had the smarts to look embarrassed.

"You heard what the magistrate said," Officer Ruo ordered. "Go back to your rooms until one of us brings you in for questioning!"

More chaos. This wasn't the right way to run a crime scene, and I knew it. Things were getting out of hand, and I needed to control the situation. If I let them leave, they could spread panic through the district. And the last thing I needed was for the Governor to get wind of it and yell at me again.

As the crowd began their slow dispersal, I let out a breath I didn't know I had been holding and sheathed my sword. I caught Ji Ping shaking his head.

"I didn't bring the right paperwork for this mess," he muttered, looking at the teeth on the ground.

"It was necessary," I consoled him.

He nodded glumly.

He was right, in a way. I shouldn't have let my emotions get the better of me. And for all my talk about putting everyone else off balance, there was something about the possibility of it being the Sickle Killer that disturbed me. A doubt gnawed at my confidence. Could my biggest triumph actually be a failure?

I watched him die. There's no way.

But doubts had a way of lingering, no matter how rational you were.

I cast my gaze across the departing crowd again, noticing the storyteller lingering at the side with some of the Red Peony staff.

"Ruo, bring that storyteller along," I said, heading for the backrooms. "I need to have a chat with him."

7

"I HOPE I CAN ANSWER WHATEVER QUESTIONS YOU MAY HAVE, Magistrate," the storyteller, Mao Gang, said with a welcoming smile. "Please, let me know how I can help."

"That remains to be seen," I said with a growl, which stopped his smile short. All things considered, he was an odd one out at this summit. His frame was slight, and his limbs scrawny. He didn't seem like the sort that knew any *wugong*. But that isn't a knock against him. He was charming and eager and had a pleasant sort of smile. Yet, there was something off about this kid—other than the fact that he liked to use my cases to spin his tales. Maybe it was because he was so infuriatingly well-mannered and showed proper respect to me and my staff, more so than the others that we'd interviewed.

No, it was because he knew details that weren't very public. That made him a prime suspect.

"It can't be him, right?" Captain Chen had said. "It would be too easy if it was."

"I agree," Ji Ping said. "What kind of idiot would linger around the crime scene and point out details?"

"Bu Yao," Officer Ruo replied.

We all winced. Bu Yao was a particularly idiotic criminal.

"Let's question him anyway," I ordered.

That was how I ended up sitting across the now cracked table in the backroom of the Red Peony. It was late in the afternoon. I was tired, my staff was tired, but the storyteller was energetic and optimistic, even with a vicious murder just around the corner.

I was in a foul mood, and despite what Officer Ruo said, it's not just because I don't trust someone that thinks I'm a good role model.

The door panel slid open, and one of the waitstaff brought in a plate of fried potstickers. I didn't offer any to Mao Gang and started eating. I could tell it was making him hungry. Mao Gang looked relaxed, eager almost. He watched my every movement with a starry-eyed wonder, even when hot dumpling grease dripped down my lips.

"So, why are you here at the restaurant?" I asked.

"I'm the Red Peony's official storyteller."

"And they just let you wander wherever?"

"Something like that," he said with a smile.

"Something? For a storyteller, you're sure short on details."

He smiled, grateful for the invitation to share his tale. "Long ago…"

"Okay, that was on me," I said, cutting him off. "How about the short version of the story?" I popped another dumpling in my mouth and made a show of enjoying it. Look, there are different ways to throw someone off their game. Sometimes, it's smashing a table in anger. Sometimes it's eating a delicious dumpling.

He smiled even bigger, and it annoyed me. "I'm glad to see you enjoying the food here. My father saved the owner of the Red Peony when I was a small child. When he died, the former *laoban*, Old Pan, took me in. When he died, I kind of bounced around from place to place until I apprenticed under

Blue Tortoise's[1] name. When I came back to An'lin, I asked for a job here, and I got it."

"That still doesn't explain why they let you wander."

"The *laoban* knows that I need space to piece together my tales. I like to blend in with the patrons of the Red Peony and listen for stories."

"You eavesdrop," I said dryly.

"I collect research," he smiled. "Sometimes that makes for good storytelling material."

"I noticed you at my speech yesterday. You looked worried."

"Well, I didn't want the fight to break the restaurant any more than they did."

He was lying. I remembered the worried look he gave the Jade Beauty and his white knuckle grip on the chair. He had a personal stake in the fight.

"I'm going to assume that you were slinking around after the fight too and 'collecting research' from the other delegates."

He nodded. "About an hour after the brawl, there was a more muted affair on the top floor of the restaurant. This one was a little more civil, but it mostly involved the Invisible Venom and the Nineteen Panthers delegations. They toasted each other and made grand apologies of their past history for accusing each other. They even invited the Luminous Moon delegation to participate. The Jade Beauty, Tian Mei, and her associate, Tang Luli, made a brief appearance but left nearly just as quickly. I don't think they liked being around Ding Enlai and Peng Ning—for all their drunken talk of reconciliation, Peng Ning was still particularly rude."

"Where were you when Peng Ning died?"

"I was in bed, asleep."

"You didn't hear anything?"

"I didn't."

"Can anyone vouch for your whereabouts?"

He looked sheepish. "Not really."

"Tell me about Peng Ning."

He leaned over the table, which creaked in protest. "As the night wore on, he got louder and drunker."

"I heard that he had a thing for the Jade Beauty."

The storyteller shrugged. "Everyone has a thing for the Jade Beauty. There's a reason why she's the most coveted woman in the area."

"And you?"

"Heavens! No."

"Why not?"

"I know my league, and she's way out of it." He laughed.

I snorted.

"You know, there was one thing that stood out to me." The young man looked thoughtful. "Peng Ning did make a pass at her. He was very drunk at the time."

That matched what Ding Enlai said.

"She slapped him—knocked him flying again. Honestly, I think he deserved it."

Another person that thinks Peng Ning deserved what he got. You were a really unlikable guy, weren't you?

"Tell me why you think he deserved it."

"Isn't it obvious? He's a creep." Mao Gang shrugged. "She knocked him flying twice in a single day, and I doubt he learned his lesson. I think she was justified."

"Why is that?"

He shrugged. "I suppose it was her way of dealing with that kind of unwanted attention."

"And do you think Peng Ning deserved to be dismembered as a way of dealing with unwanted attention?"

He blanched. "No, I don't. Maybe. I don't know."

"Which is it? You know enough about the case to have staged the murder yourself."

He grimaced. "Maybe. But I'm not a skilled enough

fighter to have taken on Peng Ning myself. To be honest, I thought it was Tian Mei."

"Why not Ding Enlai?"

"I was thinking about this. And you know, after telling so many tales, I like to think that I know my way around a good crime story. I don't think the Panther leader did it because they were old friends."

"Old friends?" From the way they were insulting each other yesterday, it was a little bit of a stretch. Then again, they did coordinate pretty well in humiliating Tian Mei.

"Sure," he said. "I'm pretty sure they staged that whole robe incident. A lot of the hot air is for show, I think." He shook his head and a frown of disgust crossed his lips. "And then there are stories about the Jade Beauty, after all. Surely you've heard of them?"

"Indulge me. Pretend I don't know anything."

He grinned even bigger than before, happy to show off his storytelling skills to his hero. "Tian Mei, the Jade Beauty, has a legendary temper to go with her equally legendary beauty. Suitors came from all across the kingdom to secure her hand in marriage, but because of her beauty, but none were found worthy. Prior to the last summit, the Luminous Moon thought it amenable to marry her off to the previous head of the Nineteen Panthers sect. It was their latest attempt at trying to make peace. But then he publicly humiliated her, gloating about his good fortune in the arrangement. He made some rude demands of her in public, if you know what I mean."

"Seems to happen a lot to her," I said, recalling the rude things Ding Enlai said.

"Well, even though he was a *gaoshou* of some importance, she broke his heart—literally. Smashed in his chest and broke five ribs and his collarbone. He recovered well enough, but then mysteriously vanished."

"Vanished? You mean he laid low?"

"No, vanished. After the incident, he made a couple of public appearances, and then was never seen again."

"What do you think happened?"

"I don't know."

"Give me a guess."

"Maybe he was too humiliated and retired somewhere? That doesn't feel right though—he would have wanted to retaliate." He sighed. "I feel bad for her. Such things shouldn't happen to her."

"Is that so?" I asked. I found it a little amusing that he was trying to put the pieces of the case together. *An amateur detective in the making.*

"It's like a curse to be beautiful in the *wulin.* Everyone that thinks they're strong becomes entitled—a beautiful woman is a prize to be won. No one deserves to be harassed like that," the storyteller said, shaking his head. "It's sad."

He had a point. The *xia* of the *wulin* were often portrayed as noble heroes, but they could be the most entitled bunch of brats this side of nobility. In a place like the martial world where strength and skill equated to power and authority, those that saw themselves as strong believed that they ruled the world. Nobility meant nothing in the way they treated women.

"I suppose her problems with that would be over if she were to marry you, Magistrate. May I offer my congratulations?"

"No, you may not. There's no marriage while there's an investigation going on."

"Yes, yes — of course Magistrate," he said hurriedly. "I hope things go smoothly."

"You tell a good story," I said, leaning back in my chair.

"Thank you."

"But you're leaving something out." I leaned close.

"Excellency?"

"You know Tian Mei."

"I know of her."

"No," I said, shaking my head. "You are intimately acquainted with her. Before the fight yesterday, I saw her smile at you, and you were nervous."

That shut him up.

"Talk."

"We were children together, long ago. I saw her briefly at the last summit and hoped that we would be able to speak this year."

"Tell me more about this."

"I'm sorry. I can't, Excellency."

"Why not?"

"It's not my story to tell."

I don't like being told no. I'd have to draw it out of him later, but I didn't want to have to torture it out of him. I thought he was a good enough kid, if a little on the annoyingly eager side.

"You know a lot about me and my cases. Why is that?"

"Is it too simple of an answer to say that I'm a fan?"

"Yes."

He leaned back in his chair. "I have a friend that works at the Tribunal. He gives me the heads up on any cases that are particularly interesting. Most of the time, they're your cases."

"That doesn't explain how you know things like the flower in the mouth."

"Ah…well…" he looked embarrassed and squirmed in his seat.

"Spit it out," I growled.

"Sometimes he sneaks me into the Tribunal. I take a look at the case files myself." He turned bright red and looked down at the table. "I guess I shouldn't be admitting to that in front of a magistrate."

"Sneaking into the Tribunal is definitely a punishable offense."

"I know. I'm sorry."

I frowned, but it was to hide a growing appreciation for the kid and how far he would go to get the details of a story right. Most of the time, people in his profession would just make it up. They are storytellers after all—factual accuracy was not their business.

He was being honest—I'll give him that. But I didn't like his answer. This was typically the point of these 'conversations' where I used to shift things from pleasant to unpleasant. In my early career, when I looked for a quick win, I'd send them off to the specialists where a proper answer would be extracted.

This time, however…

"You're free to go," I sighed.

"Really?"

"But first, one more question."

"Yes, Excellency." He perked up, eager again.

"Tell me what you know about the Sickle Killer."

His eyes widened. "You should be telling me, Sir. You're the expert here."

"Indulge me. It's been a few years and you know your way around the case. Everyone is spooked. Tell me why you think that is."

The boy was quiet for a moment, gathering his thoughts before speaking. "It's because the Sickle Killer stalked so many of them."

I waited for him to elaborate.

"From what I heard, and you can correct me if I'm wrong, everyone was afraid. He started in the Fai'ting arena and apparently something happened because the Sickle Killer left a trail of death from Tu'men to An'lin. There wasn't a real pattern to his murders. Some he just killed for fun. Others he mutilated. When he arrived in An'lin, he had a mission. He hunted specific members from the main martial sects of the city. Some thought he had something to prove—"

"What do you think he was here for?"

"Well, your case…"

"I know what conclusions I drew. I want to know what you think."

He was quiet for a moment, and it looked like he was thinking about how much he should say and whether it would be incriminating. "I think he was looking for people that wronged him. There's no record of him attending the Golden Chrysanthemum Summit, but I think he did, and I think somebody angered him. He killed nine people across the three sects before you caught him."

"Do you think that one of the sects hired him?"

He shook his head. "It wasn't an assassin. Assassins are professionals. They wouldn't let it get personal."

"And what do you think of Peng Ning's murder?"

"If it was an assassin, they did a good job of matching the way he killed." He then bowed his head. "I'm sorry if I messed up your crime scene yesterday. I was too excited to see it. I regret it now." He shuddered. "There are some things you can't unsee."

I nodded. "That's what a crime scene looks like when it's personal. An assassin doesn't take time to remove body parts and leave signatures."

"Magistrate, have you met assassins?"

I only smiled at him[2].

"Don't let me catch you sneaking files again. I want the name of your contact," I growled.

"Yes, Excellency!"

After he left, Ji Ping and Captain Chen both gave me a questioning look. I didn't like how they were aligning so frequently on this case.

"You're letting him go?" Captain Chen said. "We should have taken him in and beaten a confession out of him."

"That's not a good idea," Ji Ping added. "You can't just beat a confession out of everyone."

"And I suppose you have a better idea?" Captain Chen snapped.

"We're letting him go for now. But we're keeping an eye on him," I said, cutting off the argument before it got out of hand. My instinct said that he was being honest with me, which was more than could be said of most of the people I talked to today. "But...we're not letting anyone leave the Red Peony tonight."

Ji Ping's eyes widened. "You're keeping everyone in here? No one is to leave the Red Peony at all?"

"Nope."

"What's your play, Magistrate?" Captain Chen asked.

"I don't know yet," I admitted.

"A hunch?" Captain Chen asked.

"Maybe."

They nodded.

I was grateful they didn't ask me to explain.

"I'm not sure how it's all connected yet," I admitted. "But it's there. I think whoever we're looking for is still here."

"Wow, there's something the boss doesn't know?" Captain Chen asked.

"Must be serious," Ji Ping said.

"I said, I'm not sure how it's all connected *yet*," I snapped. "Bring me the Jade Beauty, Tian Mei. I need to have a word with her."

"Ooooh boy," Captain Chen sniggered. "Ruo is going to love this."

8

Peng Ning was an ill-mannered boor. That much was becoming more clear as my investigations continued. And while sure, he was gutsy to make a pass at Tian Mei, the famed Jade Beauty of the Luminous Moon Palace, that also made him an idiot.

Of all the martial schools and sects that call An'lin home, the Luminous Moon Palace was perhaps one of the more mysterious. I recounted what I knew about them. There were rumors that they were made up of orphans and the unwanted of the city, but those rumors were often dismissed as hearsay. They had their hands in everything, and I was fairly certain that the governor kept a mistress from the sect. As it was, there's an element of truth to every rumor. Mao Gang mentioned that he knew Tian Mei from childhood. If the Jade Beauty grew up in the sect, I wondered if she was an orphan.

The other thing I knew about them was that they supposedly had skill in multiple forms of fighting. That had to be somewhat true, given the display that the Jade Beauty put on yesterday. The truth was, no one really knew much, and if they did, they kept their mouth shut. They kept to themselves and were rarely involved in any fighting.

Occasionally, they would send a champion to a tournament, but those sightings were as rare as the emperor visiting a small village at the edge of his kingdom.

And then there were the usual rumors that they were a cult of hedonists—though I suppose that came from the minds of lustful men.

Tian Mei was the last interview of the day and from a personal perspective, one that I wasn't looking forward to at all. The famed Jade Beauty of the Luminous Moon Palace arrived at my unofficial office at the Red Peony, under the guard of Captain Chen and a dazed looking Officer Ruo.

Though I told my men to bring her alone, she entered the room with the older woman from yesterday that wanted retribution for Tian Mei's humiliation.

"Apologies, Excellency," Officer Ruo said, with a slight bow. "But Lady Tian insisted that her companion come with her."

"That's fine. Thank you," I said, dismissing him.

Ruo gave the two women a lingering look and then left.

Up close, the older woman appeared close to my age, and her beauty had not yet begun to fade. There was a familiarity there that I couldn't quite place. She bowed and smiled demurely as she entered, but I knew behind that unassuming face hid a calculating temperament. You didn't get to attend to a woman like the Jade Beauty if you were an idiot, after all.

For her part, the Jade Beauty certainly lived up to her reputation. She strode in with all the confidence of fifty men and settled in the chair across the table, casting an imperious gaze over me. It was enough to make me question who was really in charge here. By all accounts, she was an incredibly beautiful woman and a rare jewel not seen in a hundred years of beautiful women. I didn't know about that, but she was certainly one of the most striking women I had ever seen.

I didn't realize how young she looked—at first glance, I could have easily been her father if things had played out differently in my life. Then again, there were also rumors that the Luminous Moon had developed cultivation techniques that could mask their true age and present a mask of youth to the world.

This is who my wife wants me to add to the family? How did she even get involved with these people?

I knew that any half a dozen men would have wanted her, desired her to be theirs. But the moment I locked eyes with her, I knew she was trouble—the kind of trouble that either leaves you broke, broken, or breakfast for worms. From her angry and petulant look, I could tell she was someone used to having things done her way. She fixed me with an impatient glare, and she snorted at my questioning stare. I've rarely dealt with a more hostile suspect.

We were well beyond disaster territory here.

Ji Ping brought in a pot of tea and began pouring two cups —one for me and one for Tian Mei. When he was done, he bowed and left, leaving me alone with these two women.

"You are Tian Mei," I said.

She nodded once.

"Do you know why you're here?"

She nodded again.

"You should address her as Lady Tian Mei," the older woman interrupted.

"And what should I call you?"

"Tang Luli."

"And who are you to *Lady* Tian Mei?"

"She's my *baomu*," Tian Mei explained. Given her apparent age, it made sense. A *baomu* was a governess of sorts; a handmaid, friend, and mother figure all baked into one. I wondered at that and her need for her presence. While the Jade Beauty was young, I thought she was too old to be constantly accompanied by a *baomu*. *Maybe the baomu was now a servant?*

"Ah, so you do speak," I said with a thin smile.

She clicked her tongue in annoyance, as though irritated that she had been tricked into answering a simple question.

Tang Luli spoke up. "Magistrate Tao Jun is the special investigator for the governor."

"Hmph."

"He's also the husband of Shao Lan," she said. "You know, the one Shao Lan spoke about in the deal with the elders of the sect."

Deal? What did that woman get me into?

"You're Shao Lan's husband?" Her eyes widened, and she cast a piercing look over me, looking me up and down. Eventually, her lips turned into a sneer as she found me unimpressive.

"That I am," I said with an amused chuckle. "Not a great first impression for either of us."

"Ugh," she said, crossing her arms and leaning back into her chair. She looked out of the window.

Ugh, was right, I thought. A pretty face, yes, but I don't know what my wife saw in the young woman. She was decidedly unpleasant. Maybe that's what she saw in her—an unpleasant person to make my life more miserable. It made sense, in a sick sort of way. After all, isn't marriage just a game of seeing how miserable you could make each other until you die?

The natural order of things.

And people wonder why I hang out at the Tribunal office all the time.

"You should answer his questions, Lady Tian," Tang Luli said. "It'll make things easier for us."

"Yes, you should," I said. "You are a suspect in Peng Ning's murder."

"Ugh. Fine," Tian Mei complained. "But I'm only doing it for Shao Lan."

"That works for me." I shrugged, leaned across the table, then fixed Tian Mei with the best intimidating smolder as I could manage. "Tell me about the little altercation you had with Peng Ning last night."

Her eyes widened momentarily. "You know about that?"

"It's my job to know what happened to him...especially since he's dead."

"It's a good thing he's dead," she sneered. "What a despicable man."

"Why do you say that?"

"Isn't it obvious? He's a lowlife that humiliated me yesterday. It's a good thing he's dead. If he tried a third time, I would have killed him myself."

I raised an eyebrow. "I don't think that's something you should say to a magistrate."

"So?" she snapped. "I'm innocent. I had nothing to do with it."

"So?" I said, using her snappy tone. "I have no reason to believe you." I leaned back into my chair. "Tell me why exactly I should believe you. Out of everyone I've talked to today, you have had the most reason to kill him."

"If the young mistress says that she was not involved, then she was not involved," the *baomu* said. "She honors her word. She doesn't retaliate."

"It doesn't work like that. You can't just say I'm innocent and have it all swept away," I retorted.

"Men like that," Tang Luli began, "always seek to dominate those around them. Women aren't people to them. We're just objects to be possessed." She shuddered. "Or passed around."

I grimaced. She had a point.

"Were you in An'lin when the Sickle Killer was murdering people from your sect?"

Tang Luli nodded, and when she spoke, her words were slow, as if remembering a past she didn't want to recall. "I was there the night he killed Lai Xue. I heard a commotion in her room and I entered to see if she was okay." She took a deep breath to control her emotions. "He grabbed me before I knew what was happening and held his sickle to my throat." She pointed at a thin scar on her neck. "He threatened to kill me but for some reason let me go."

She was a potential victim? I wondered, and then it occurred to me why Tang Luli felt familiar. I remembered Lai Xue and remembered finding her body mutilated. Lai Xue was the final victim of the Sickle Killer, and I had already figured out his identity. As a result, Tang Luli was deemed an unimportant witness. I lost her in the aftermath of the case, but seeing as how we moved to execute the killer, it didn't matter at the time.

"You were lucky," I said.

She nodded, and a single tear rolled down her face before she regained her composure.

"And you still haven't answered my question," I said, turning my attention back to the young woman.

"Yes, I struck him last night," she said like a sulking child.

"Is that all you're going to say about it?"

"Hmph," she snorted.

I crossed my arms and waited for her to give me details. I let the silence hang between us, and for a few moments she was fine with it. But as the heartbeats turned into moments and minutes, and then into eternities, I saw her begin to squirm. She tried to hide it with indifference, but seeing how impatient she was when she first entered the room, I knew this was the perfect thing to break her.

Here's the thing about me—I have no problem waiting in silence. As a magistrate, silence is probably one of the most powerful tools I have. All I have to do is sit and glower and let the moment drag out. Before long, most people end up breaking themselves. They just can't handle the silence. It works especially well on young people.

Like the Jade Beauty.

"He propositioned me," she said finally. When I didn't say

anything else, she continued. "He was drunk and stank of liquor, and he wouldn't take no for an answer. Then he made another grab for my...in front of everyone..."

"My lady, I don't think you need to continue," Tang Luli cut in. "It's not proper."

"I can speak for myself, *Baomu*. The *magistrate* wants to hear about it." She shook her head, then turned an angry glare at me. "Anyway, the minute he touched me, I had enough."

"And then you pounded the qi out of him," I said. "Impressive."

"It was only one strike."

I raised an eyebrow. "One move?"

"Lady Tian Mei is famous for her move, The Touch of the Almighty," the *baomu* said with some pride. "You saw it in action yesterday."

Tian Mei smiled a deadly smile.

"Isn't it just a glorified slap?"

"I dare you to say that again to me," Tian Mei glared.

"It's a slap. Tell me, where is the lie?" I said.

"You—!"

It was so easy to disrupt this girl. Completely used to getting her way, she did not deal well with people contradicting her. In an odd sense, she reminded me of Lady Yue[1], one of the most powerful noblewomen in the city.

"Aiyah, Lady Tian, you shouldn't threaten the magistrate like that. It's not polite. He can't help being ignorant about your power."

"Stop smothering me, *Baomu*!" Tian Mei snapped again. "You should have stayed in the room."

My wife wants to kill me, I realized. *That's why she wants me to marry this one.*

"Apparently, your little slap broke a lot of chairs."

"I went easy on him."

"I also heard you had a scuffle with the previous leader of

the Nineteen Panthers as well. Destroyed his chest. He hasn't been the same since."

"I didn't go easy on him," she said with a dark smile.

"You have a habit of destroying men?"

"Only men that deserve it."

"And how often do men deserve it?"

"Most of the time," she said with another deadly smile.

"In fact," I added, "he's missing, presumed dead. Do you have anything to do with that?"

"He's dead?" Tian Mei asked despite her feigned disinterest. "What happened?"

"You tell me," I replied. "You were the last one to have fought with him."

"Hmph," she snorted. "If he's dead, then he deserved it as well. *Biantai*[2]."

"Lady Tian Mei acted out of self-defense," Tang Luli said. "It was an appropriate response. You men of the Tribunal wouldn't be giving this much scrutiny to it if it was Peng Ning that fought Ding Enlai, would you?"

"Actually, I would," I lied. She had me there. As equal as the *jianghu* tended to be, the Tribunal was not so open-minded. When it came to breaking the law, there was significantly less wiggle room for women. It was a bias that was as ridiculous as it was stupid. Anyone worth their martial skill in the *wulin* knew that women were just as capable of destruction and death as the men. Still, that didn't stop the Tribunal from its prejudices.

She fixed me with a flat look. We all knew I was lying.

"What do you know of the storyteller?" I asked Tian Mei.

"Mao Gang?" she said with some surprise.

"You know who he is?" I raised an eyebrow.

As though realizing her mistake, she didn't answer, instead fixing me with an imperious glare.

"Who is he to you?"

"If you're implying something…" Tang Luli threatened.

I raised my hands in a placating gesture. "I'm merely going through the facts of the case. And there are some questions I need answers to, that's all. Now if Lady Tian Mei would please tell me how it is she knows Mao Gang?"

"We grew up together," she said tersely.

"I thought you were raised by the Luminous Moon Palace?"

"After a certain point. I knew him from before."

"Where?"

"Here in An'lin."

"What happened?"

Instead of answering, she looked away. Tang Lulin answered in her stead. "The Luminous Moon Palace takes in orphans and castaways from all tiers of society. There was a time when they were both in their care."

"So then, you're quite familiar with him?"

"I haven't seen him in years."

"Was it a joyful reunion then, to see him here at the Summit?"

She shrugged.

"He was hoping to speak to you," I said, watching her carefully for a reaction. "Oh, you should have seen it yesterday—he was so worried when you were about to fight Ding Enlai and Peng Ning."

"Is that so?" she said casually.

I fought the urge to smile. Her apparent indifference was a facade—that much I could tell. Beyond her show of annoyance and arrogance, she was the type to hide her true feelings.

So she and the storyteller know each other, but they've both tried to keep this relationship secret. I remembered the thin smile she gave him, and thinking about it now, it was the only smile I've seen her give in the last day. *Were they lovers? Was it that easy?*

"Are we quite done here?"

"Do you have somewhere to go?"

"I'm in no mood to answer trivial questions."

"Questions in a murder investigation are hardly trivial," I said with a grim smile. "It's not looking good for you, Lady Tian Mei. Two men dead in your wake. And you've admitted to striking the victim the night before he died and we have your very public fight with him at the beginning of the summit. This doesn't help your case."

"So, what then? Are you going to arrest me?" Her eyes were full of petty defiance. *Where is this anger coming from?* I wondered.

"Should I?" I asked. "You really haven't done anything to persuade me not to. For all I know, you are the Sickle Killer. You slit Peng Ning's throat and removed his hands. You made such a bloody mess," I said, shaking my head. "Blood everywhere. Officer Ruo, the one that escorted you here, vomited, that's how bad of a mess you made. You then made your meaning very clear by writing that message on the wall. The *laoban* of the place doesn't appreciate that, you know."

Sometimes you throw out wild accusations and see what sticks. Sometimes it works, and sometimes they confess.

"That wasn't me," she said. She looked sick.

"Magistrate Tao Jun, please spare us such details," Tang Luli said. She, too, looked a little pale after my graphic description of the scene.

I don't think my tactic was working today.

I turned my attention to the *baomu*.

"And where were you last night when the murder happened?"

"I was asleep."

"And Lady Tian Mei can confirm that?"

"She was asleep before I was."

"So no one can confirm your alibi, then?"

"Don't you bully my *baomu*," Tian Mei interjected.

"Or what?" I said, turning an icy glare to the young

woman. "As a suspect, you're in no position to make demands."

"Hmph," she retorted.

"You know, it's easy for me to interpret your lack of cooperation as guilt. I've arrested people for less than that."

"Aiya, the wise magistrate couldn't do that," the *baomu* said. "He doesn't have enough proof."

"I don't need proof to throw you both in the dungeon of the Tribunal."

"The governor would have something to say about that," Tang Luli replied.

I bit back a curse. I shouldn't have allowed the *baomu* in the room—no matter how much of a stink the young woman would make. Guess I was a little flustered by a pretty face. I'm getting sloppy. An appeal to the governor would make things complicated.

I cast a glance at the Jade Beauty and the *baomu* at her side. As a pair, they were unlikable, and yet I had a growing hunch that somehow Peng Ning's death had something to do with her. The threads were there but so fine as to be almost invisible, impossible to grasp—like catching spider silk with a chopstick.

"What are you hiding, Lady Tian Mei? What are you refusing to tell me?"

"I have nothing more to say to you."

"It doesn't matter. I'll find out one way or another."

Ding Enlai, Tian Mei, and Storyteller Mao Gang. Could either of these three be the new Sickle Killer? There was, of course, the thought that the original Sickle Killer was back, but I didn't want to go there. I supposed the easiest way to tell who it was would be to arrest them all and torture them long enough to get a confession out of someone. But knowing the governor and all the scrutiny this case was drawing, I needed to be careful. If word got out that we not only had a serial killer on the loose, but the Golden Chrysanthemum

Summit was disrupted because his magistrate was interrogating delegates, he'd have it in for me.

Yeah, my life would get considerably worse.

Could be a good way to retire, though.

"You are not to leave the Red Peony tonight. Do you understand?"

"Of course, Magistrate," Tian Mei said as sweetly as possible. "As you wish."

I fought the urge to roll my eyes. Hot and cold. One minute, the sweetest woman in the kingdom. The next a cantankerous sore—and one with a deadly repertoire of attacks.

Forget Peng Ning: this is all an elaborate way to murder me.

I rose from my seat and slid the door open to let Tian Mei and Tang Luli out, but no sooner had they exited the room, when I heard the guffaw of Ding Enlai.

I couldn't hear exactly what he said, but I heard the Jade Beauty's response.

"For the last time, the answer is no."

"Come on, Tian Mei, let's go out. I'll show you a good time," Ding Enlai said, reaching for her hand. His arrogant smirk had returned. "Don't be such a prude."

"I said no." Tian Mei twisted out of his grasp.

"Geez, you're such a stuck up bitch. Can't you take a joke?"

I frowned. In a weird sort of way, this was a special moment to be savored: an idiot was about to get what he deserved. And whenever that happens, you should take some time to relish in it.

Moments like this stump me. As a magistrate, I wanted to intervene and tell Ding Enlai to get lost. It's never a good look to see a woman harassed by a scumbag, and in any other circumstance I would. But Tian Mei and Ding Enlai were both murder suspects and clearly had some history. Letting them interact might reveal something interesting.

Against my better nature, I decided to hang back and observe what happened. After all, every investigation comes with a web of lies that binds everyone together in a net of misery. If there's one safe assumption I could make, it's that no one is telling the entire truth. Given the history of the three sects and the Golden Chrysanthemum Summit, there was another assumption I could make. Everyone was connected somehow, and they don't want those connections to be public.

"Don't you touch her," a voice called out from down the hallway. I craned my head to the side, and to my surprise, it was the young storyteller. His expression was dark, and he folded his arms across his chest. Given the size difference between the Mao Gang and Ding Enlai, it would have been hilarious, if not for how tense everyone was. I was a little surprised. The storyteller didn't appear like the sort that would get involved—especially as someone that didn't know wugong.

Ding Enlai seemed surprised to see the storyteller at first, then grinned wickedly at him. "Or what?"

"You leave her alone," Mao Gang repeated.

"You're not going to touch Lady Tian," Tang Luli added as she moved between Ding Enlai and the Jade Beauty.

"No one asked you, or you," Ding Enlai sneered at the *baomu* and the storyteller. "This is between me and the *lady*. You were previously engaged to the head of the Panther Sect. As that is me now, I think that engagement still stands. You're mine. Someone needs to teach you your place."

I wasn't even going to think about how that logic worked.

"She's not some brothel wench you can proposition," Tang Luli continued. "She's a *gaoshou* of the Luminous Moon."

"I can handle this, *Baomu*," Tian Mei said.

"Don't you insult her like that!" the storyteller said.

"Mao Gang, please don't get involved," Tian Mei said.
They definitely knew each other.

"My Lady, you should just ignore this type of scum…"

"Stop telling me what I can or can't do, *Baomu*. I can handle it myself," Tian Mei insisted.

"Who are you calling scum?" Ding Enlai said. "Don't you know who I am? I am Ding Enlai of the Nineteen Panthers—the most powerful sect in the *wulin*."

I fought the urge to roll my eyes. The Nineteen Panthers were at best a mid-tier sect with aspirations beyond their station. He clearly had an overinflated sense of his own importance.

"Then you'll understand my response," Tian Mei said. With a sudden lunge forward, she swung her hand back and then slapped him across the face, sending him flying backwards. He crashed into the wooden paneling of the wall behind him, splintering it with his impact. "Isn't that how you say 'no' in the *jianghu?*"

The Touch of the Almighty. This was the second time I had seen it in action. On the one hand, it was a glorified slap, though one with the force to make a warrior monk weep with envy. By every definition of the word, it was a slap—an open palmed strike pulled back with power to hit a target. On the other hand, it was no ordinary slap. It was a glorious fluid motion that seemed to transcend color and light and the nature of the universe. I wondered at her ability to channel her qi, the amount of force she was able to generate with such little movement.

"Do you call that *just* a slap, Magistrate?" Tian Mei said without looking at me.

On the *other*, other hand, it was still a slap. I kept that thought to myself. I didn't need to fly into any paneling myself today[3].

A wide-eyed Mao Gang stood gaping in the hall.

"Pick up your jaw, kid," I said. "You might start drooling."

The storyteller shook himself but still stared at Tian Mei, his expression vacillating between shock and admiration.

"Aiyah, *meimei*," Tang Luli chided. "It's not ladylike for you to do things like that."

"I don't need you to protect me, Luli," Tian Mei snapped back. "I'm not a child anymore. I can take care of myself."

"Aiyah, but you shouldn't do such things in front of the magistrate! He could arrest you."

I shrugged. "He deserved it."

"No one asked you, Magistrate," Tian Mei said, storming away.

"Tian Mei!" Mao Gang called after her.

"Lady Tian," the *baomu* said, hurrying to keep up.

"Owwwww," Ding Enlai groaned as he tried to sit up.

"Maybe you should proposition her again. See what happens. You might get lucky." I walked past without helping.

THE COOL NIGHT BREEZE WAS LITTLE COMFORT TO MY increasingly foul mood. It was late, far later than I was usually out. I had been wandering aimlessly through the Long'cheng district. I wasn't worried about anyone mugging me around here. In fact, as irritated as I was, I was hoping for another fight. Striking Thinning Hair guy felt so savagely good, and it would be great to aggressively work through some of my frustration on some poor unsuspecting bandit.

Summer was nearly here, and I could feel it in the way my robes were starting to cling to my body. The air was as thick as water, humid and cloying. The streets still, the bustle of everyday life, slowing for the bliss of sleep. It was the deep night when I found Lao Wang in his usual space in the garden. I chased away the birds that occupied the bench and sat down next to him.

I was frustrated, despondent, and a little anxious as I tried to process the day's events.

Earlier in the evening, I visited the Tribunal office's special collections department. The Tribunal likes keeping artifacts of interest. I remembered they had held onto the Sickle Killer's weapons after the man's execution. As far as weapons went, they were a pair of unique pieces. While collapsible weapons were not entirely uncommon, a collapsible sickle was unlike anything I have ever seen in the *jianghu*. They could fold into small metal cylinders, barely large enough to be hilts, but still retain every bit of their deadliness.

Thinking I could learn something from the weapons that might help me in this case, I sought them out.

Unfortunately, they were missing.

The poor clerk in charge of the collection had no idea where it went and apologized profusely to me. Ji Ping might have given him an earful—as my adjutant, the man craves order and if anything is out of place, he has a fit. When he has a fit, no one, not even me, is safe from his wrath.

Missing weapons is definitely cause for a fit.

The thing was, the sickles didn't make any sense. The Golden Chrysanthemum Summit was a gathering of some of the best fighters in the *jianghu*. Anyone could have killed Peng Ning with their martial skill—why use the sickles? And who could have taken it? It wasn't like the special collection was under a lot of protection, so it could have been anyone.

I sighed. They were questions with no answers at this time.

"You know what I wish, Lao Wang? I wish I could have gone undercover at this thing right from the beginning—no fancy speech, no nothing. I could have worn one of my disguises, told everyone that I was Jin Min[1] and no one would have known[2]."

Lao Wang was silent, but I could tell that he disagreed.

"Yeah, I know what everyone says about my flashy outfits, but it would totally have fit in with the summit[3]. Then I'd be on the inside, and I could figure out what exactly was going on here."

Lao Wang was an old friend, a trusted confidant that I

could open up to without any judgement. He always listened to me, never offering any judgment; his expression was always solemn and expressionless no matter how much I cursed or yelled around him. He was always still, the perfect paragon of patience and understanding.

Though his facial expression always appeared wise, he never shared any of his wisdom directly, instead allowing me to work through my own thoughts and discover the answer for myself. His stone face a deep comfort to me. I knew I could always count on him to be there for me, no matter the hour of the day or night, storm, sun, or blizzard.

Lao Wang never let me down.

I sighed again and stretched out next to him.

"What am I going to do, Lao Wang?"

He didn't answer. But I wasn't expecting him to. As always, he merely responded with perfect peace and stoicism.

Oh, did I mention he's a statue?

He's a statue.

Not *like* a statue. He *is* a statue. It's not a metaphor.

Years ago, when I first arrived in An'lin, I discovered Lao Wang on a case. After that, I started coming to visit him on the regular. There was something about being near him that felt reassuring. In an odd sense, it reminded me of Master Guo from my days at Blue Mountain, though Lao Wang wasn't likely to hit me with a stick if I said something ridiculous.

Still, Lao Wang's silence could be both encouraging and damning. He offered both vindication and criticism. Today, I needed Lao Wang more than ever, so I sought him out after investigating the crime scene at the Red Peony. He wasn't too far away and Lao Wang was waiting with an expectant ear.

How nice it is to have an old friend to talk to.

Was it really the Sickle Killer? It had to be a copycat. My mind fixated on this question and churned my thoughts in its wake to the point where I had a hard time separating my fear and anxiety from my methodic examination of the facts.

If it was the Sickle Killer, I absolutely had to catch him. My professional pride wouldn't have it any other way.

Mao Gang, the storyteller kid, had a lot of facts right. Peng Ning's murder was so similar to the Sickle Killings eight years ago that it could have been done by the same hand. I couldn't believe I didn't notice it right away. It chafed at my professional pride that some young punk like him noticed it.

The original Sickle Killer was a martial arts expert of some renown. He was a prominent member of a sect that has now faded into obscurity, a champion without equal. In fact, at one point he was an undefeated champion in the Tu'men Fai'Ting arena until Thunder Hand Zhang Lei defeated him in a thirteen round match.

Defeated, the man lost all sense of control and humanity. No one knew it at the time, but he killed the master of his own sect and then began his killing spree. A revenge killing on those that he thought showed him disrespect.

Oddly enough, he steered clear of Zhang Lei. Perhaps he was scared off by the person that defeated him, or maybe because Thunder Hand was the honorable sort that treated everyone with respect. I suspect that true sense of honor might have saved him in a way that damned the others.

The killings began in the winter. He stalked prominent members of the Invisible Venom, Nineteen Panthers, and Luminous Moon. He killed three from each sect, each murder more gruesome than the last. Let's just say that the crime scenes disturbed more than a few officers of the Tribunal. It's not every day that you see victims dismembered and displayed in horrific ways. Each victim was an accomplished martial hero in their own right—they all had reputations in the *jianghu* for being good at what they did.

Mao Gang said that there wasn't a real pattern to the murders, but that was where he was wrong. Though they came from different sects and had different fighting styles, they all shared one thing in common: they were all liars.

I don't mean liars in the way that a conman tries to sell you some qi-strengthening tonic and says that it's also good for getting rid of that rash in that place you don't want to tell anyone about. And I don't mean liars in the sense of a street urchin that's willing to tell you anything you want to hear for a small fee. No, I mean it in the worst way possible—they were men and women that held up one face to the world and revealed another in private. They may have been good people on the outside, but they were like cheaply made pottery. Chip away at the paint to reveal a crumbling counterfeit.

Were they good people? No. Were they bad people? Also no. Did they deserve to die? Don't we all for something or another? Sure, no one is innocent, but no one is entirely evil or good either. The best we can really hope for is to do enough good to outweigh the bad and maybe, just maybe, we can make it into the next life without too much punishment.

Maybe.

But they were hypocrites. They were the kind to praise you to your face and then stab you in the back. When I investigated their backgrounds, I found all kinds of dirt on them. The nine victims were all part of a secret cabal of their own—one involved with slavery of children and other less than savory activities. As gruesome as the killings were, there was a sick sense of justice at play here, one that matched some unknown morality.

Pretty soon, the murders became known as the Sickle Killings, named after the "chicken claw" sickle he used to kill each of the martial artists. As far as weapons go, the sickle is a rare one—it gave him an advantage. And somehow, even when they knew he was coming, they were unable to defend against him.

I was a young man at the time—new to the Tribunal. I wanted to make a name for myself, so I took on the biggest case I could find. They all laughed at me, but I was angry, impetuous, and I wanted to prove something to myself, to everyone.

I was such an idiot.

I think if I were faster, if I were smarter, there'd be less dead bodies—people that would never see their loved ones again. If I weren't so arrogant, maybe I would have been able to pick up on the clues sooner and saved some people.

As it was, I goaded the Sickle Killer into making a series of mistakes, and I was able to lure him into a trap. In a thrilling display of swordsmanship, I managed to slice the tendons of his sword hand and kicked him off the roof of a building. I was fortunate enough that he fell and knocked himself unconscious, rather than dead. The Tribunal made short work of him after—sentencing him to death in a very public execution. The martial schools and sects of An'lin were grateful that such a disgraceful villain had been apprehended. I was a hero. This was the first of a series of big wins that defined my career in the Tribunal, my fast track to becoming the governor's favorite—and yes, I'm fully aware of the pull my father had in that, but hey, I did a lot of hard work too!

I watched the man die. He was dead. But as irrational as it may have been, I felt a stab of panic that he might, in fact, be still alive. Someone that was supposed to be dead, not actually dead? Yeah, it wasn't the weirdest thing ever. I mean, faking your own death was a great tax dodge.

"Lao Wang, we have a copycat killer," I said, trying to sound sure of myself. "It's not nice to have to deal with ghosts of the past."

Lao Wang was silent.

"You're right, Lao Wang. I can't treat it like the old case. This is something different—I can't let my old biases get in the way." I sighed, leaning back on the bench beside him. "I have to work the case."

Peng Ning was murdered. His throat was cut by a sickle

and hands removed. It was one of the grisliest crime scenes I've seen in years, and it was clear that it was the work of someone with an intense dislike of him. They took their time to mutilate him. Yet, because there were no signs of a struggle, he might have known the person that killed him.

I had three suspects in the murder of Peng Ning: Ding Enlai, the leader of the Nineteen Panther Sect; Mao Gang, the Red Peony's storyteller; and Tian Mei, the Jade Beauty of the Luminous Moon Palace. Beyond those three, the *baomu*, Tang Luli, was also a person of interest.

Out of these three, only Mao Gang appeared to have any ties to the Sickle Killer. He knew how the killer operated and his behavior. He said he learned those details from studying my case files, but he also could have been the right age for an apprentice. Yet, my sense of him was that he didn't know any martial arts, and I'm not usually wrong about that. On top of that, there didn't appear to be any connection between Mao Gang and Peng Ning other than that confrontation in the hall. Was his worry over Tian Mei enough to drive him to kill a man and remove his hands?

Tian Mei had the most motive to kill Peng Ning, having been assaulted twice in a single day by him. She had shown her temper and her strength three times in the last day, attacking Peng Ning twice and Ding Enlai once. Were they unprovoked attacks? No. Did they deserve it? Probably.

Was she our killer?

I didn't think so either. Her manner was far too blunt and direct. It didn't match Peng Ning's methodical dismemberment. She was more likely to burst into the room and beat his face in than to slit his throat and kill his goons.

And then there was Ding Enlai. As lecherous as Peng Ning and clearly a man without much self-control, could he be our killer? Given what I had seen of the cowardly way he tried to exculpate himself of any wrongdoing, it wasn't likely as well. Like Tian Mei, he was a blunt force, confident in his own abilities as a fighter. And while he had a dislike for Peng Ning, he didn't have enough of that hatred to dismember the man. He also looked genuinely spooked by the Sickle Killer—even if it was a worry over his manhood. At any rate, a trait that set him apart from Mao Gang and Tian Mei.

As for Tang Luli, the woman hovered over Tian Mei like an overprotective parent. She certainly had the motivation, but did she have the killer instinct? She remembered the terror of the Sickle Killer, and if she could be believed, she had almost been killed by him. From the way she spoke of the incident, I could see she was clearly traumatized. Was the damage severe enough that she would emulate the trauma she faced and inflict it on others?

And what to make of all the bickering and fighting over the Jade Beauty? Between Peng Ning and Ding Enlai, she had a beautiful woman's unfortunate ability to provoke lustful catcalls and harassment. And perhaps it was her 'delicate' nature, but she also inspired people like Mao Gang and Tang Luli to jump to her aid as well. And that didn't account for the effect she had on Officer Ruo and the others.

No answers. I was missing something.

I sighed, thinking back to the fight at the beginning of the summit. Maybe that was the key—that was the last time I saw everyone in a room together and saw how their web of relationships tied them all. Peng Ning and Ding Enlai never wanted to fight fair or equally with the Jade Beauty.

That was the problem.

Me? I don't care one way or the other. If you're good, you're good. If you're strong, you're strong. And if you could break my face with a single punch? More power to you! You deserved to be at the top of the martial world. That was why I had nothing but respect for a woman like Bai Jingyi. Strong, intelligent, and possessing of a keen business instinct that would make most merchants envious—she was truly formidable.

But women were never equals in the eyes of men like Ding Enlai and Peng Ning. They were objects to be owned, less than human. Even with the threat of the Sickle Killer around, Ding Enlai was *still* stupid enough to harass Tian Mei.

If Tian Mei did kill Peng Ning, could I really fault her for wanting to be treated as an equal? After all, I myself had killed men for far less than respect.

"I hope this doesn't spread. It'll cause panic," I muttered. The way my growing anxiety battled with my instincts made it clear that there was a race against the clock here.

"I can take the rest of the night off, right? I need some sleep. I've got everyone secure in the Red Peony. We have lots of guards in place, and Officer Ruo and Captain Chen are on site. They can handle it."

Lao Wang didn't answer, but I think he agreed with me.

"The problem is, I have no idea who this new killer is. Last time, I had some idea, and it was just a question of injuring his pride enough that he wanted to fight me. This time around, we're starting from scratch."

I could sense Lao Wang's disapproval.

"I know. I know." I held up my hands in a placating gesture. "Work the case."

When in doubt, work the case—that's the advice I first got from Magistrate Bao when I first got my position. The old man had worked in the Tribunal since before Emperor Xia took the throne and was basically on his way to ascending to the heavens as an immortal when I arrived in An'lin. I didn't listen to a lot of what he said—I thought he was a bumbling old fool—but he did give me at least one good piece of advice that has stuck with me throughout the years.

A murder rarely happened in a vacuum. Sure, there were killing sprees where innocents were slaughtered for no reason, but those are more war crimes than anything else.

Murders don't just happen. They're the result of people, and people make mistakes.

"It's up to me to tug on the threads until I find the right one," I said, rising to head home.

Lao Wang approved.

THE NEXT MORNING, ANOTHER AMBUSH AWAITED ME.

"Good morning, husband," my wife greeted with a cheery smile.

I frowned. Something was up. We normally kept to ourselves, maybe exchanging a few grunts of acknowledgement at our morning meal. I had another long day ahead of me, and her good mood was so far out of the norm that it immediately put me on edge.

"Hello, wife," I said as nonchalantly as possible. Look, I have to play it cool or else hell will consume us all. She who rules the manor with an iron fist is temperamental at best[1].

"How was your day at work?" she asked. "You were home late last night."

Now I knew something was really up. She never asked about my day. In eight years of marriage, I could count on one hand the number of times she asked about my day.

Look, our marriage was about as resentful as you could make it. She resented me, and I resented her. We were both unhappy people stuck in a marriage that tied our families together in a way that we ourselves never wanted. And the end result, was that we had a son together so that we could continue the cycle of misery.

Why disrupt that balance of unhappiness with cheeriness?

"Is there something I can help you with, wife?"

"I merely wanted to see how my husband's day went."

I fixed her with a flat look. "There was a murder."

"Oh my."

"A very gruesome one."

"Oh my."

"Blood everywhere."

"Please, just stop," she said, shaking her head. I got a sick satisfaction from seeing her pale and then immediately felt guilty about it. She didn't do anything to deserve that, no matter how tyrannical she may be. She walked over to the door panel and slid it to the side. The first light of day spilled in, opening a view of the garden. The garden and its courtyard are my favorite parts of the manor. Big enough to get lost in[2], it featured all the little trappings that said you were in a noble household—a weeping willow with long tendrils that dipped into the stream, a stone bridge and a charming gazebo, carefully manicured shrubbery and flowers, a pond stocked with koi and other charming fish, and, of course, a row of cherry blossoms that filled the garden with delightful pink florets in the spring.

You know, the usual stuff.

The scene always brings a certain sense of peace to me, and today was no different. I took a deep breath, let the scent of the morning air soothe my nerves and my growing anxiety. We wouldn't be able to keep the incident under wraps for long, and if the people found out...

"It wasn't a good day yesterday, and I'll likely be away for a while investigating this," I added in a more conciliatory tone.

"I see," she said. "Well, thank you for letting me know."

An awkward silence fell between us for a while. It was

now my turn to squirm. I racked my brain trying to think of something to say, anything to say, as we stood gazing out into the garden.

"I...uh...met Tian Mei, the Jade Beauty," I said finally, then almost immediately regretted it.

"Oh?" She immediately perked up, though she tried to play it casual.

"She's an interesting one," I said, matching her casualness.

"An interesting one?"

"What do you want me to say? She's incredibly beautiful?" I said dryly.

"She is, isn't she?" she said in a tone that bordered awe. She turned to look out at the garden of our manor. Then she added, "Do you think she's the one for you?"

"What are you talking about?" I probably could have phrased that better. After spending the last day thinking about her as a murder suspect, being reminded that she was a candidate for marriage was jarring, to say the least.

"I'm not going to repeat myself," she said with that no-nonsense tone.

"I think it's way too soon to make any kind of decision about that," I said. I was about to add that she was at the center of a criminal investigation, but that didn't seem like the right play. "What's your deal with her, anyway? I don't understand why you would want someone like her in our household."

"What do you mean 'someone like her?'"

I weighed my words carefully. Calling her out for being a brutish person that was likely to kill me was definitely not the right way to go. "I mean, don't women get all defensive and protective of their place in the pecking order? Aren't you afraid she might replace you?"

"Is that all?"

"Huh?"

"Tian Mei and I are…" her eyes took on a distant look, "We're good friends. We go way back."

How far back could they go? Tian Mei looked young.

"Friends?"

"We have an understanding."

"Uh-huh."

"Hmph, you wouldn't get it."

Maybe she was right. Maybe I don't understand. The machinations of this woman were as opaque as red lacquer. Then again, I never really tried to understand her. The thought gave me a stab of guilt, like maybe I had been taking this she-demon for granted and not seeing her for who she really was.

Who was I kidding?

There was nothing to get—only malevolence and a desire for my complete and utter destruction.

"You can't just do this one thing for me?" she asked quietly. Her eyes bored into me. I knew that look—it was one of earnest pleading before adroit manipulation. Things were going downhill fast. A part of me thought that I should try to stop it, but I didn't care. There are some things you just can't fight.

"How is getting another wife a 'thing for you?'"

"I want companionship."

"At what cost?" I said. "I've done some background on her. She's a dangerous woman. She's likely to kill me with her martial skill."

"She's no danger to anyone that treats her well," she said. That, in itself, was a thinly veiled threat. As though I needed to treat Shao Lan better as well. What more could she want? All the servants answered her every command. She lived in a luxurious manor in the prestigious Long'cheng part of the city and had all the wealth she could need.

What more could she want?

Companionship?

"You don't know how hard it was to even be considered for a match. The Luminous Moon Palace are very selective of who they would negotiate with, and you're lucky you're on the list. She's one of the most desirable women in the An'lin." She shook her head. "No, the entire kingdom. People would kill to have her," she said.

"Wait, what did you say?"

"What? How desirable she is? Isn't that obvious?"

"No, no, the other thing."

She clicked her tongue in annoyance. "She has no family, so the Luminous Moon Palace is responsible for her matches. You're just lucky that you have a good enough pedigree to be considered…"

"No, not that—the other, other thing."

"People would kill to have her?"

"Yes, that!"

"Hmph," my wife sneered. "You would focus on that. It's always death, death, murder, murder, kill, kill with you. Who is dead today? Who killed who? It's like death follows you everywhere you go."

"Never mind that," I snapped, cutting her off. "What do you mean by people would kill to have her?"

She sighed, as though she were speaking to a really stupid child. And maybe I am a stupid child that needs things spelled out for me.

"Don't you remember the story of Tiao Chan? Men fought battles and killed hundreds because of her."

I frowned. Tiao Chan was a historical figure from the distant past of the previous dynasties. The prime minister of the time was a wicked and cruel man that was backed by a fearsome general with no peer. Tiao Chan's father, a patriot aware of the cruelty and corruption of the prime minister, sought a way to depose him. Tiao Chan volunteered herself for a 'beauty trap' to drive a wedge between the prime minister and the general. She ultimately succeeded, though the argument between the two men over who had claim to Tiao Chan lead to a bloody conflict that claimed the lives of hundreds and saw a kingdom nearly collapse. [3]

"You really think Tian Mei is like that?"

"Hmph," Shao Lan snorted. "Shows what you know. The Luminous palace doesn't give out the title of Jade Beauty so readily. It's only given to someone whose beauty is unmatched. The history of that title is a blessing and a curse. It's an elevated position, yet it causes conflict everywhere they go."

"Conflict. And you want to bring that kind of person into our house?"

"Well…" she stammered, suddenly flustered.

Conflict everywhere they go? I froze. The sentence wormed its way into my brain, digging through the noise of all my other thoughts. Could it be that the Sickle Killer was someone that had a claim to owning her?

"What's wrong with you?" she asked, frowning as she noticed the dumbfounded expression on my face.

"Nothing," I stammered. "Nothing is wrong. But I need to go back to work. I just realized something…"

"Back to work. Back to work. I have no husband. You're married to your work," she sighed, making a dismissive gesture with her hands. "And you wonder why I need companionship."

"Yes, yes, you need a companion. I get it. I get it."

"And what about breakfast?"

"No time!"

"You have to eat something."

"I'll eat when I'm dead!"

"That doesn't even make sense."

I hurried out the open door and sped through the garden, ignoring her trail of complaints.

11

I CLUTCHED MY SWORD, JOY, IN MY HAND AS I RAN DOWN THE streets. It trembled in anticipation, as though it knew it was going to get a taste of combat. I don't really know how to describe it, but there are times that it feels like my sword has a mind of its own. There are times when it was almost hungry for blood, eager to fulfill the purpose for which it was made. Joy was one of a pair—one of the lost treasures of Blue Mountain. Its sister blade, Sorrow, was in the care of my sworn brother, the legendary swordsman Li Ming.

Sorrow and Joy were never meant to be separated like this, but well, Li Ming and I haven't been great at preserving our sect's lost legacy. Probably because most of what made Blue Mountain great has been destroyed for the last fifteen years. We were the only two swordsmen left—though I've often tried to implore my brother to take on apprentices again.

I mean, I guess I could, but since he was the senior disciple, it's his responsibility. And I'm a magistrate! I'm far too busy with other things to do it.[1] I don't need more crap to do.

It was early. The streets were mostly empty and the

commerce of the Long'Cheng district hadn't begun to flow yet. I ran as quickly as I could to the Red Peony. With no crowds to weave through, the journey took less than five minutes.

A pair of city guards slouched outside of the restaurant and jerked to alertness when they realized who I was. I brushed past them and into the restaurant, ignoring their greetings.

"Hello?" I called out.

Within a moment, a servant of the Red Peony greeted me and said that the restaurant was still closed and I should come back later.

"Do I look like a customer?" I snapped, waving my magistrate token in his face. Sometimes you need to flex your imperially mandated authority.

"Forgive me, Excellency," the servant bowed immediately. "I should have recognized you right away."

"Get up, you fool," I said. "Where is Ding Enlai?"

"The leader of the Nineteen Panthers? He should be in his chambers," the servant said, puzzled.

"Take me there now."

I needed to talk to Ding Enlai again before it was too late. The wife had stumbled onto something that may have been the missing piece to this case. Yesterday, Ding Enlai said something about being entitled to the Jade Beauty because she was engaged to the former leader of the Nineteen Panthers. It stuck with me and was digging into me the wrong way.

"You're mine now. Someone needs to teach you your place," Ding Enlai had said.

As we drew closer to the room, I noticed the quiet and emptiness of the hall. Where were the guards? I specifically told my staff to set up a watch on Ding Enlai, and Officer Ruo said he'd take care of it himself. He and the other guards were nowhere to be found.

I smelled the iron tang of blood before we arrived.

Oh no.

The servant knocked politely on the door. I glared at him.

"We don't have time for this," I said, reaching for the door and slamming it open.

A person cloaked and hooded in black stood over Ding Enlai's body. I couldn't make out if they were male or female and they wore a mask that hid their features. And in one hand...

A sickle!

For a moment we stared at each other, the confirmation of it being a sickle killer rooting me to the ground. My eyes darted to Ding Enlai's body. He was already dead, that much was for certain. One hand had been removed, the other still attached but bloody.

"He will not touch anyone ever again." They flicked their weapon and a splash of blood hit the ground and the paper panels of the door. The servant behind me peeked around the corner, saw the killer, and let out the shrillest scream I've heard in a long time.

As though that were a cue, everything happened at once.

I unsheathed my sword. Joy rang out with a clear tone, its white blade a glow in the dim room.

"Stop!" I yelled, which, of course, was the wrong thing to do. One of these days, I should sneak up on a killer and just arrest them like that. Maybe tap them on the shoulder and yell, "Surprise!" and then arrest them. It would certainly make things easier. Instead, I yelled something stupid like STOP at them, which everyone ignores.

They turned and ran. With a quick slash of their sickles, they cut through the door paneling that led from the room and into the courtyard gardens.

I followed closely behind and nearly caught them with my blade before they turned at the last minute to let my sword cut a ribbon off their cloak. My weapon must have nicked them, because they grunted and spun around. They gave a flourish of their free hand and a metal handle slipped out of their sleeve. With a sharp click, it unfolded itself into another sickle.

There was no doubt—these were the original Sickle Killer's weapons.

I unleashed a flurry of strikes before they could get in position and was rewarded with a cut on their arm that bled instantly. They hissed in irritation, then redoubled their assault. A distant memory triggered from when I fought the original Sickle Killer. I needed to be careful not to let my blade get caught by both sickles. Last time, I was caught off guard and disarmed by a strike.

There it was!

The second sickle swept out to catch my blade and twist it out of my hands. I had hoped that it wouldn't be the same technique—the ramifications of that development were a little too frightening for me to think about at this time. Could it really be the same person? I slid my weapon backwards, leaping up with a qinggong assisted jump to land on the eaves of the Red Peony. Seeing an opening, the Sickle Killer leaped up and onto the edge of the stone wall, running along its edge before jumping onto the roof of the adjoining building.

I cursed.

It was going to be a chase.

I hated qinggong chases.

Look, fighting someone of any level of skill is hard enough without qinggong. Qinggong made things complicated. Using lightness Kung Fu meant that they were well trained, and could turn any battle field into an aerial fight as well. A qinggong user tended to have less powerful techniques— opting to use their qi for agility rather than strength. Unfortunately for me, the Sword of the Nine Dragons *jianfa* focused more on speed and quickness and less on agility and flying through the air, so qinggong wasn't my specialty. Still, I wasn't a complete novice, and I held my own and chased them across the roof.

Qinggong chases were happening in my life at an alarming frequency as of late. And I wanted no part of it. It was a young person's game. Or, oddly enough, an old master's game—the number of old masters I've seen chasing each other through treetops was kind of astounding.

But seeing as I was neither a young person nor an old master, but rather a magistrate approaching middle-age at a pace I was not comfortable with, this was not a situation I wanted to be in.

They bolted, gliding over roof after roof of the Long'cheng district. I gave chase as best as I could manage. One of these days I was going to chase after someone on the street level, and we'd just settle things by talking, and we'd have some tea and a few laughs and then I'd haul them to jail. Is that too much to ask for?

Apparently so.

With enough of a lead, they began throwing roof tiles at me as I ran. I dodged what I could, took a couple to the chest, which really hurt. I caught the fourth tile they threw at me and launched it towards them. I didn't think I'd get them, but I got lucky. The tile hit them square in the back as they ran, knocking them off of a roof and into a courtyard.

I followed them down. They were sprawled on their back and struggling to stand up when I arrived. I scanned our environments quickly. The enclosure was modest, a small yard of stone tiles and a large ceremonial altar with burning incense at the center of it. On the opposite side of us, high brick walls lined the edge of the courtyard. They looked tall enough to challenge most qinggong practitioners, which meant that I had them trapped.

What a wonderful day.

"You've got nowhere to go. Let's just have a chat, shall

we?" I stared at them. A trickle of blood dripped down their hand, covering their fingers.

"Magistrate Tao Jun," they said. Their voice sounded far too young and high-pitched to be the man I captured ten years ago, and even though I knew that the man was dead, the confirmation was a small relief, but it didn't answer how they fought the same way as the original. "I have nothing against you. Stay out of this."

"Oh no," I replied. "The last time I listened to a villain as I was chasing them, I got in so much trouble for it. And not to mention the paperwork. Months of it[2]." What was it with villains that wanted to warn you from getting in their way? Wouldn't it have been easier for them to kill me instead? I mean, I don't want to die, but that's a better way of getting people to stay out of your way, isn't it? "You're not the Sickle Killer, but you're using his weapons. What should I call you? The Sickle Baby?"

"Stay out of this," they repeated.

"Look, Sickle Baby," I said. "I don't even know what 'this' is? Why'd you kill Ding Enlai? Why did you kill Peng Ning?"

"I only killed them because they deserved it."

Well, at least there's one confession.

"So you did kill them," I said.

They stiffened, realizing their mistake. "Yes."

"Why the sickles? Who are you?" I asked. I snapped my fingers. "I know who you are. You are the Jade Beauty."

"She has nothing to do with this!" they shouted angrily. "Leave her be!"

Taken aback by the response, something clicked in my head. I saw another angle to this. "She's going to be *my* concubine. She's going to be *mine*. What do you make of that?"

"She won't be yours."

"No, she won't be *yours*," I retorted. I felt like I was in a childhood disagreement over the affections of the local pretty crush. I was too old for this crap. "What, you think that killing someone that harassed her will make her fall for you?"

"She won't be anyone's. If you touch her in any way, I'll end you."

"Ooooh, a threat to the magistrate. You know that's a crime, right?" It wasn't—at least not really, but they didn't know that. No one really knew that.

"Enough of this," they said, throwing down what looked like a round ball. It bounced and hissed and within seconds, the courtyard filled with a thick gray smoke. Over the sound of the smoke, I heard the sound of the sickle clanking against the wall. I coughed, waving my hands to try to clear the smoke as I chased after him. But with my vision obscured, I didn't see where the wall was and ran right into it. Not a very elegant move, I know. I'm glad no one was around to see it except for the birds[3].

"What's going on out here?" someone yelled, as they emerged from the building adjacent to the garden. "Who are you?"

"Official Tribunal Business," I coughed as I reached for the pendant at my belt. "Nothing to see here."

Truly nothing to see here. After a chase, I still didn't know who our killer was, but in a roundabout sort of way, my list of suspects had shrunk. The slight frame. They spoke in a voice that was either high for a man or low for a woman. Could it be the storyteller or the Jade Beauty? I felt a sense of relief wash over me. It wasn't the same Sickle Killer as before. He hadn't miraculously survived his execution.

At least I had some confirmations: the Jade Beauty was at the center of this.

Either way, I had another murder on my hands and a determined criminal.

What a wonderful day.

WHAT ELSE COULD GO WRONG? I WONDERED. BY THE TIME I MADE my way back to the Red Peony, the restaurant was in a state of utter chaos. Guards tried to keep delegates from leaving, while upset staff wept and murmured in all corners of the restaurant.

Worst of all, Officer Ruo was down. They found him stuffed into an alcove behind a child-sized vase full of bamboo. He wasn't dead, thankfully, just unconscious. Still, no one was able to rouse him until Ji Ping found a particularly potent smelling piece of stinky tofu. A couple of waves of it under his nose and the idiot had the gall to lick his lips as he struggled to wakefulness.

Delicacy or menace, stinky tofu definitely had its uses.

"What happened to you?" I asked.

"I...don't know. Someone got me."

"Someone in black with a hood, wearing a mask?"

"I don't know," he shook his head. "They got the jump on me."

I sighed. I didn't think it likely that Mao Gang could have taken out someone like Ruo. Could the Jade Beauty have done this?

"What's going on?" he mumbled. "I'm hungry."

"How can you think of food at a time like this?" Ji Ping hissed. "That's going to change when you see the corpse."

"Huh?" He moaned.

"Ding Enlai is dead. The Sickle Baby got him," I said.

"What? Dead? How?"

"How do you think?" I sighed.

"Wait, Sickle Baby? Is that the new nickname?"

"I'm still testing it out."

"I don't like it, boss," he groaned. "It's terrible."

"Hush, you don't know that. You're still groggy," I scowled.

Ding Enlai was dead, and it felt like that was on me. If I had detained everyone at the Tribunal, then maybe Ding Enlai would still be alive. To be fair, I wasn't as upset about his death as I was about my gamble. I took a risk, and it didn't pay off.

At least we had some kind of proof it was the Sickle Killer, or at least the Sickle Baby—the copycat. That much I knew. Maybe I was too stunned by the possibility of someone coming back from the dead (it wouldn't be the first time it happened to me), and I was making stupid mistakes. I cursed to myself. I couldn't afford to keep making mistakes like this.

How in all the demon bureaucrats of *diyu* did everything go wrong here? We set up guard patrols around the Red Peony. There were guards on the inside. Officer Ruo and Captain Chen were all in positions inside, keeping watch. And whatever else I may say about my people, I know I could count on them to keep watch. Despite his big size, Officer Ruo was no slouch, either. He knew how to acquit himself well in a fight.

This wasn't a slip up for them.

This was done by someone or someones in the Red Peony with a high level of *wugong* to be able to go about undetected.

I waved a guard over, told him to find a healer to take

care of Officer Ruo. I waved another guard over and told them to secure the Jade Beauty and Mao Gang, the storyteller. I then walked down the hall to the crime scene. Ji Ping and Captain Chen were already there, both looking slightly pale and grim.

The room was similar to the one Peng Ning occupied, only this one didn't have gore everywhere and had no cryptic message splattered on the walls. A small table occupied the corner of the room, and a meal had been laid out. Over the iron tang of blood, I caught a whiff of the Red Peony's crab dumplings. In spite of myself, I felt my mouth start to salivate, and I remembered I didn't have a morning meal today.

What? Of course, I wasn't tempted to eat the dumplings. Dumplings by a corpse? That's gross. I have some standards, you know. And they could be poisoned[1].

Our Sickle Baby friend didn't have a chance to arrange Ding Enlai's body, and his corpse slumped on the ground, dropping from the chair the killer was working from. On the table next to the body were a pair of chrysanthemums blossoms—the killer's signature ready for marking.

One hand had already been removed.

He'll never touch anyone again.

It's the touch that's important.

Did he deserve this? If it were possible, he was even less likable than Peng Ning. I took stock of my emotions. Was I sad about this? I didn't think so, but I didn't like that he died on my watch. Look, I've seen a lot of death. Some people deserve it. Some don't. The best way to do it was to not feel anything for anyone. At least that's the way I'd like to play it. It doesn't stop me from getting dragged into some idiotic chase, thinking that I could stop the tide of death. Maybe it's my own ego. The dead man slumped on the floor, staring accusingly at me.

"I'll get to the bottom of this," I said to myself.

From the other side of the room, I heard a gag and Officer Ruo retch.

"That's two you owe us, Ruo!" I called out.

"Uuuuuugh," came his reply.

I missed it earlier when I confronted the killer, but Ding Enlai wasn't alone in the room. From the colors of his robes, it looked like another one of the Panther delegation. He lay in a pool of his own blood, his hair splayed out around him. His throat was slit with a deep slash—the sickle blade again.

Killed like an afterthought. He was just in the way.

Captain Chen crouched over a third body in the corner—a young woman. She looked like one of the Red Peony's staff. A pretty enough girl, likely brought in by Ding Enlai to relieve his earlier 'frustration.' Another innocent victim in all of this.

"She's dead," Captain Chen said, shaking his head.

The girl coughed.

Captain Chen and I exchanged a surprised look, then he hurried to cradle her and help her wake.

"Come on, kid, wake up," he said as gently as he could. The permanent frown on his face softened a bit as she stirred.

The killer left the girl alive but killed the other Panther. It was like the murder of Peng Ning and his companions. Anyone associated with the sect was a target.

Ji Ping cleared his throat at my side, which was my cue to pay attention to him.

"Coroner is mostly done with his examination of Peng Ning's body," he said as I turned to him.

"What did he find?"

"Traces of paralysis poison."

"We'll probably find it in him too, then," I nodded towards Ding Enlai's body. "Get him working on this one."

"Yes, Excellency."

I closed my eyes, clearing my mind to look for patterns of qi around me. When I opened my eyes, I found no traces of any major expulsions of qi. A few faint traces around the body of the other member of the Panthers but nothing around Ding Enlai. No bruises from *dianxue*[2] to paralyze or kill. This was good old-fashioned blade work.

Well, good was relative.

The only other traces of qi were at the back of the room where I began my pursuit of the sickle killer.

I frowned.

"I know that look," Ji Ping said quietly. "You're thinking of something."

"The Sickle Baby had the opportunity to paralyze both Ding Enlai and Peng Ning."

"Sickle Baby?" He raised an eyebrow. He wasn't a fan of my new nickname. He never liked my nicknames[3]. He shrugged. "There's something I'm not understanding here— why did he kill the Panther, but leave the girl alive?"

"When I arrived on the scene, I saw the killer."

"You actually saw him?"

"Them. It could be male or female," I corrected. "Anyway, they said something along the lines of 'he will not be touching anyone ever again.'"

"So this was specific to Ding Enlai," Ji Ping nodded. "And the other Panther was just collateral damage?"

"Just like with Peng Ning and his men."

"He must be referring to the brawl at the beginning of the summit."

"They," I corrected again. "I'm not sold on the killer being a man. And the incident after I interviewed Tian Mei."

"This is personal for *them*. And *they* kept the girl alive," Ji Ping nodded towards the young serving girl from the Red Peony who still struggled to wake. Captain Chen spoke to her in a calm, reassuring tone and was carefully positioned to block her view of the dead bodies. I fought a smile. I didn't know he had it in him. "Why?"

"Ji Ping, what kind of contracts do the Nineteen Panthers and the Invisible Venom have?"

My adjutant straightened, and his eyes took on a distant look as he recalled the facts. Beyond being good at his job, Ji Ping also has an amazing memory. He can recall facts and details that most people would require copious amounts of notes to remember. Copious.[4]

"Officially, they have government contracts in some caravan escorts and guarding some noble families." He frowned. "The city guard also hires them to take care of bandits from time to time," he added with some disgust. It was no secret that Ji Ping didn't like people from the *jianghu*. He often thought they were more trouble than they were worth.

"And unofficially?"

He leaned in close. "You won't find this in any of the official records, but I believe the governor uses them to maintain a hold on the illicit goods trades."

I raised an eyebrow. "Illicit goods?"

He shook his head, "People."

"Still? You'd have thought the Sickle Killer killing their people years ago would change their minds about that," I shook my head. "That would explain why the governor wanted us to keep the Panthers happy." While the buying and selling of people wasn't entirely illegal, it wasn't entirely legal either. Years ago, Emperor Xia issued an edict declaring slavery forbidden and the trade of people illegal. However, most provinces never executed that law, and the imperial court never followed up with anyone, so the trade continued. The governor's official stance matched the imperial court, but behind closed doors...

Well, he had to get rich somehow.

I looked at the severed hand of Ding Enlai.

He will not touch anyone ever again.

Could this have been the work of Mao Gang or Tian Mei? Both disliked Ding Enlai and Peng Ning. Both thought that they deserved to be killed. On top of that, Sickle Baby sounded furious when I taunted them about the Jade Beauty.

Maybe this isn't just a revenge killing for their lecherous behavior. Maybe it's about ownership?

By now, Captain Chen had the serving girl sitting up. He gestured for me to come over, and I squatted down by her side, careful not to let my silk robes touch anything dirty.

"Did you see what happened?" I asked.

"I didn't," she said.

"Tell me what you remember. Be quick about it."

She seemed startled at my tone and spoke in a fluster. "Earlier in the day, Master Ding asked me to come to his chambers. I said no, of course."

Seeing her here in his chambers, this was clearly a lie.

"Then why were you here?" I asked wryly.

"Well…" she blushed.

There were rumors about the Red Peony—sometimes it acted as though it were like a pleasure house. I thought it was hearsay, nothing more, but maybe there was some truth to it. Like I said, they were known for their discretion and their ability to take care of their clients. If their clients required a little extra company, they provided it as well. Everyone turned their heads away, and no one was to ever speak of this.

"I came in and he offered me a drink. I don't remember much after," she admitted.

"Was the drink drugged?"

"I don't know, sir."

"Did you see who came into the room?"

"I was already falling asleep when there was a knock on the door," she said, struggling to remember. "Everything was a blur. I couldn't really see."

"Think."

"It sounded like he knew them."

"Who was it?"

"I don't know," she stammered.

"Tell me!"

"I don't know! Oh, please protect me, sir," she sobbed, clinging to Captain Chen.

Captain Chen cooed reassurances that she would be okay.

I sighed. Another dead end.

The guard I sent to fetch the Jade Beauty, and the storyteller returned alone. "I'm sorry, Excellency. Lady Tian Mei refused to come out of her room."

"How dare she?" Ji Ping snapped. "Did you tell her it was not a request?"

"I did, sir," the guard quivered. "And storyteller Mao Gang is nowhere to be found."

"What?" I asked, surprised. Ji Ping and I exchanged a look.

"You don't think…?" Ji Ping asked.

"Get a group together and look for him."

"And the Jade Beauty?"

"I'll go see her myself."

13

———————

MOST OF THE TIME, EAVESDROPPING IS A SOCIALLY FROWNED upon activity. Anyone's grandmother will tell you that you need to respect other people's privacy. Of course, that same grandmother will probably then eavesdrop on a private conversation between you and your best friend and then report back to the rest of your clan about the scandalous stuff you got yourself into.

Eavesdropping—A socially unacceptable, accepted practice[1].

But sometimes, if you're lucky, you might accidentally eavesdrop on a conversation that's important, which is what happened shortly after I left the crime scene to think. On the way to the Jade Beauty's room, I heard her voice speaking in a low whisper. I ducked behind a particularly large pot in an alcove to listen.

"They're saying Ding Enlai is dead," she said.

"He is," another voice said. Was it Mao Gang? "It was the Sickle Killer again. Same as what happened to Peng Ning."

"Good riddance," she sniffed. "The Sickle Killer is doing us all a favor by getting rid of that scum."

"Tian Mei, you can't say stuff like that. They think it was you," the other voice said. It was definitely Mao Gang.

"Stop telling me what to do. I swear you're as bad as *Baomu*," she snapped.

"We're just trying to keep you safe."

"We're not orphans anymore. I don't need you both to keep me safe. I can keep myself safe," she hissed. "I trained hard so that I didn't need anyone to keep me safe and then you all want to put me on some pedestal, like some piece of art, to be admired!"

"Shhh, keep your voice down."

"You're doing it again!"

"I'm sorry," he whispered. "Please. I think they're looking for me."

They were silent for a moment. I don't know what they were doing. Maybe looking into each other's eyes? Maybe glaring at each other? I don't know—I couldn't see around the pot.

"Is it really the Sickle Killer?" Tian Mei asked. "*Baomu*'s stories—they make him sound terrifying."

"Maybe that's the point," Mao Gang replied. "Something to scare Peng Ning and Ding Enlai."

Either they were innocent or they were great at faking it. I continued to listen for any other clues.

"Why do they think it's you?"

"I know things about the Sickle Killer."

A pause.

"That's not all, is it? You do know something."

Mao Gang continued his silence.

"It doesn't matter. You need to get out of here before they find you," Tian Mei said.

"But you're a suspect too. You have to leave."

"I'm an important delegate. They can't touch me."

I rolled my eyes. *We'll see about that*, I thought.

"Did you kill them?" she asked in a low voice.

"I didn't kill him!" Mao Gang protested.

"Am I supposed to believe that? You told stories about the Sickle Killer. If anyone could duplicate his crimes, it's you!" she said anxiously. "Why would you kill on my behalf? I told you I could protect myself."

"I didn't kill him," he insisted again.

The floorboards creaked as they left.

I was about to follow them when I heard a familiar voice behind me speak. "Ah, the so-called Hero of An'lin. I knew I would find you skulking here instead of doing your job. I can't say I'm surprised."

Startled, I rose and turned around. A man in a blue robe uniform that matched my own stood in front of the pot, gloating like a little bully who just claimed a treat from an innocent victim.

"Magistrate Ku[2]," I said dryly. "How nice to see you too." From down the hall I heard the scampering of footsteps as Mao Gang and Tian Mei ran. I bit back a curse. It was just getting interesting.

"The governor wants to see you," he said.

"Can't it wait? I'm in the middle of a case," I snapped.

"No. He wants to see you now. I'm here to bring you in."

"Bring me in? What am I, a criminal now?" I scoffed.

"Your days of flaunting the rules are over," he sneered. "If I could, I'd arrest you right now and I'd take you the Tribunal. The things I would do to you…"

"I don't think that came out the way you wanted it to," I grimaced. Magistrate Ku had a way of making innocuous sentences come out really weird.

"You—!"

"You need to make sure you find Mao Gang," I said, cutting off his outburst. "He knows something about the killer!"

"Get going," the man hissed instead.

14

I DIDN'T DO ANYTHING WRONG, AND YET, MAGISTRATE KU WAS treating me like a criminal. He practically shoved me out of the Red Peony. Officer Ruo and Captain Chen looked like they were going to attack him, but I waved them off. There would come a time when they could do that, and I would gladly punch Ku too. Today was not that day.

Oh, but I really wanted it to be today.

Just one punch—POW—right in the nose.

I could die a happy man.

A *very* happy man. Magistrate Ku was an idiot.

It wasn't that long of a walk to the governor's palace, but it sure felt like a long and lonely one. All of these walks feel long and lonely when you know an earful is waiting for you on the other end.

Even though Captain Chen and Adjutant Ji Ping offered to come with me, I told them to stay behind. I appreciated the gesture, but this was my own responsibility to bear the brunt of the governor's anger. Instead, I told them to keep working the case. I needed them to find our storyteller friend, and I needed them to see what I wasn't seeing.

As it was, getting dragged to see the governor like this

was also not a fine moment and another tally on an otherwise increasingly bad day. Sometimes the world feels like it's crumbling and falling apart around you, and all you can do is put on a smile and just grin and pretend everything is okay.

Ji Ping tells me that's far too cavalier an outlook, but he's wrong.

We all have bad days, and I'm no exemption. Getting ambushed by my wife and being told I needed to marry someone else so she could have *companionship?* That's pretty bad. But then getting dragged like this to see the governor like I'm some sort of criminal and not a high-ranking official? On the grand scale of disaster, catastrophes, and cataclysms, today was getting up there.

Just grin.

Another death. And even though I didn't like Ding Enlai or Peng Ning, I couldn't help but feel like it was my fault. I wasn't smart enough, fast enough, to see what was in front of me. And I still wasn't seeing what was in front of me. Maybe I was so overwhelmed by the appearance of the Sickle Baby that I kept thinking it was Sickle Killer from before. Or maybe my ego was getting the better of me.

Just keep grinning.

I screwed up. Maybe I shouldn't have let them all brawl at the beginning. Maybe that made things worse. Maybe I should have detained everyone in the Tribunal to keep them away from each other, even though that would have likely pissed the governor off even more than letting them go free. While all this nonsense was happening, a killer was on the loose, and somehow Mao Gang and Tian Mei knew more about it than they were letting on. There was no right answer here, and the choices were already made.

I felt the smile on my face start to slip.

The anxiety grew inside me, and I knew what was coming. Maybe it was another reprimand. Maybe I'd get kicked off the case. I don't know. And that's it, isn't it? Not knowing was an uncertainty that spoke to the dark place in all of us—that spot where nothing but the doubts and insecurities that plague us exist and want nothing more than to consume us whole. Because the true fear, the dark one that whispers to us in the scariest part of the night or in the deep moment of the soul where you wonder if it's all worth it, that darkness, that all-encompassing despair that wants to drown you, will swallow you up completely if you let it.

Sometimes the fear is so real that it actually hurts. And the worst part is that it taps into all those other emotions that I keep buried underneath all that bluster and smile, and general good humor. Regret. I saw my mistakes. The day Li Ming and I left Blue Mountain with Sorrow and Joy, leaving Master Guo Yang and the rest of the sect defenseless as they fell under the Black Tiger General's blade. I tell Ming all the time that it wasn't his fault. But maybe it's my fault.

It's totally my fault. If I had said no, if I hadn't let him talk me into it. Maybe we could have saved them. Or we could have ended up dead next to them. That's the thing about regrets, isn't it? It only paints one not so rosy, entirely overcast view of the future. Maybe things would have been different. Or maybe they would have turned out completely the same. Or maybe they would have turned out worse.

And then anger. There's always anger lurking underneath that fear. Anger at myself. Anger at the world. Anger at all the injustice in the world that I couldn't prevent. All the lives I've taken in the name of the emperor, the men and women who have died under my Joy, the villages that I've burned, the times I've had to close my heart to the suffering of others because it would have just been too much to take.

Maybe there's something to this regret.

My father got me this position. Sure, I tested well enough in the imperial exams that I could have gotten a ministerial post in the capital, but who wants that? I had my choice, so I picked a nice magistrate position in the middle of nowhere. I thought I'd live out my days in quiet.

But Father wouldn't have his son confined to some backwater, oh no. The minute my two-year term was up, he pulled some strings and had me reassigned to An'lin. He somehow made sure that I was in the governor's august company. No one would ever confirm it, but I had my suspicions that the assignments I got early on were because of him.

Maybe if I had just said no. If I had been strong enough to stand up against my father, things would have been different. Maybe I could have had the life I wanted, instead of the shadow of what my family wanted. Maybe I wouldn't be stuck in a marriage with a woman I barely loved, with a son that doesn't want me as a father, with another marriage looming overhead like the shadow of carrion. Maybe if I screwed things up badly enough, everyone would leave me alone and I could lead the life I wanted.

Maybe maybe maybe maybe.

Maybe.

Fat chance.

Somewhere along the line, this had become my life. And now there was a certain sense of professional pride here on the line. The truth was, I wanted nothing more than to hide in bed. Maybe not bed; my wife could find me at home. Maybe I just wanted to run away and be a wandering vagrant. I'd panhandle my way across the jianghu, without a care in the world. No case. No wife. No threats of marriage.

It almost sounds nice, doesn't it?

But the problem with an escape fantasy like that (and I have many of those), is that you're never able to actually escape. Sure, you run for a little bit but then it always comes to find you again. Sometimes when you least expect it.

The only way forward is through. And going forward

means that you have to take your lumps when you're the one at fault.

An angry glare. That's what greeted me in the governor's study. As I crossed the room to bow and give my greetings, it seemed to me that the governor was upset and even more on edge than usual. Something was off, and I didn't think it was just the murder. There were rumors that said his home had been raided by the Black Tigers, but he would not confirm it, nor did he want any of us to look into it.[1]

Like I said, we all have our secrets.

Magistrate Ku followed me in and took up a position at the Governor's side, gloating at me the entire time. The governor gave him an odd look but ignored him otherwise.

"I, Magistrate Tao Jun, greet you, Excellency," I said, bowing and throwing on my full formality.

"Hmph," he grunted.

"Might I ask if everything is okay? You are upset," I inquired. In hindsight, maybe I shouldn't have called attention to his mood.

"It's not okay! Between the Black Tiger Rebellion and your screw ups, it's a miracle the entire city isn't burning!" he said, slamming a hand on his desk.

Maybe just a little upset.

"You're an absolute idiot!" he yelled.

Well, I guess there was no mincing words today. "Sir if I can explain—"

"No explanations, Tao Jun. I told you that I wanted things to be quiet before the Golden Chrysanthemum Summit and instead what do we get? The whole town is talking about the murders. Murders! First of all, you let them fight each other before the summit began. And now the leaders of the delegations are dead! I swear if anything happens to Lady Tian Mei, I'll have your head!"

"I thought it would be best…"

"I'm talking here, Tao Jun. I'm talking," he all but shouted at me.

"And now rumors are spreading all around town about the reappearance of the Sickle Killer."

"How did those details get leaked? Everyone was under strict orders not to say anything." That caught me by surprise. I may have been a little sloppy on this case, but I wasn't *that* sloppy. Out of the corner of my eye, I caught the grinning face of Magistrate Ku.

And then I knew. That bastard sabotaged me.

I was so naïve. I thought he wouldn't pull this kind of crap.

I was so wrong.

And now he was just raking it all in.

Enjoy it while it lasts, you bastard.

Maybe the governor was right. Maybe it *was* all my fault. But if that was so, then I needed to make it right.

"I thought you caught him. How is he still alive?" the governor accused.

"I did catch him, and there's no way we executed the wrong person."

"Then how do you explain this?"

"Governor, I know I can solve this case." I cupped my fist and bowed deeply to him, but even as the words fell out of my mouth, I felt doubt creep along my spine, that familiar feeling of irrationality. *I watched him die. It's not him. It can't be him.* "Please give me another chance. I know I can do it. I've almost figured it all out."

"No, Tao Jun, you're too close to this. The whole town is talking about the Sickle Killer, and if it really is him."

"That's why I need to be the one to take him down." I

didn't bother telling him that it wasn't the same guy. "You know me."

"I do know you, and that's why I say you're too close to the case," he said, and there was a lot of sympathy in his eyes. "Look, you did good last time. But maybe you're just not seeing things clearly enough right now. Besides, if you're supposed to marry the Jade Beauty, then you shouldn't be investigating her."

How did everyone know about this supposed marriage?

"Go home. Go see your wife. Take some time off," the governor cut me off. "You've been working too hard lately. Magistrate Ku will take over."

"Yes, Excellency," I said, bowing again. My heart sank.

"Thank you, Governor," Magistrate Ku said, bowing. "I will bring this murderer to justice."

The idiot couldn't bring his mother to the market if he had a map and a servant dragging him by the hand, let alone bring a murderer to justice.

"I know you will," the governor said. "Dismissed."

15

I DID WHAT THE GOVERNOR ORDERED. I WENT HOME. I SAW MY wife. And after I saw her, I immediately went to my study. No matter what anyone may tell you, I was not sulking for a week, nor was I feeling sorry for myself. The fact that I didn't leave my house or my study, for three days does not speak anything to self-pity or a bruised professional ego. Not at all. And no matter what anyone says, I was NOT hiding in my study from my wife.

Absolutely not.

In fact, you're crazy for even thinking it.

And whatever anyone else might say, the servants did not have to drag me out of my study to go back to the Tribunal. That's just undignified, and that wouldn't happen to me. They certainly weren't ordered by Ji Ping to do so, though, now that I think about the smug smile on Shao Lan's face, it must have been a joint effort. Who is really in charge around here?[1] I am. Me. I am in charge.

The Golden Chrysanthemum Summit went ahead as planned, though it was an understandably muted affair. The Invisible Venom and Nineteen Panthers left the day after Ding Enlai's murder, before the official opening of the summit. Suffice it to say, they were spooked by the murders of the heads of their delegations. The Luminous Moon Palace, tired of the scrutiny and the harassment they faced at the hands of the other delegations, withdrew to their own headquarters in An'lin.

The governor gave a big speech. He tried to soothe the nobles and the other citizens of the city, claiming that his best people were on the job. That was obviously a lie because we were sitting on the sidelines, and Magistrate Ku's people were NOT the best. Still, the governor's speech worked and didn't work. People went on with their lives, perhaps a little more cautious than usual.

In the end, only a handful of delegations from the distant parts of the area showed up. Apparently, they hadn't heard the news about the murders and the Sickle Killer. When they showed up, they were spooked and opted to attend the summit during the day and spend the night elsewhere. Whispers about the Red Peony emerged—stupid ones. "The red isn't for prosperity, it's for blood."

People even began calling it the Sickle Peony.

Like I said, stupid.

That idiot Magistrate Ku kept working the case. And, of course, he immediately jumped to the wrong conclusions. I don't like Magistrate Ku, but I certainly don't wish him the worst[2]. I wasn't expecting Magistrate Ku to make the same or worse mistakes than I did, but he did, and he made them worse. He's an idiot, so everything blew up spectacularly like firecrackers on Lunar New Year. He pulled the Jade Beauty in for an extensive interrogation, which, of course, drew the wrath of the Luminous Moon Palace. Their advocates sent down a litany of complaints to the governor, who quickly axed that idea.

Magistrate Ku wasn't wrong. The Jade Beauty was a thread of this investigation that needed to be explored. To him, it was obvious that the murderer was the Jade Beauty, despite the fact that she didn't fit the profile. She wasn't a victim or a target, but she was central to all of it. As the most obvious answer, he went with it. Making very public arrests and loud accusations of the prize of one of the most influential sects in the city was decidedly NOT the way to do it.

In the end, he turned up no leads, pissed everyone off, and the governor yelled at him and apparently, it was quite the earful, and everyone within earshot ran away and couldn't believe how angry the man was. Thankfully, because I was 'off the case,' all the blame and scrutiny fell on Magistrate Ku. The nobles eviscerated him, wanting to know what he was doing to keep them safe. The governor then booted Magistrate Ku off the case and tried to bury it in the name of keeping the peace. He lied to the nobles, saying that it had all been resolved and everything was fine.

Better him than me, I guess. There's only so much kowtowing and apologizing a man can do before he loses all sense of his own dignity. But what do I know? I was just in my study for that time. It's not like I had spies and assassins report to me on what was going on in the city. Who would do that[3]?

Things just have a way of working themselves out.

Adjutant Ji Ping, Captain Chen, Officer Ruo, and I moped around our office at the Tribunal. Even though this was my loss, my squad felt it too. A week later, they were still talking about the case as though we were still on it. They were determined to figure out what we missed and bring a close to the investigation, even though we had all been unceremoniously booted off it.

"I still think Mao Gang was the one who did it," Captain Chen said. "The storyteller ran away after Ding Enlai was murdered. If that's not a sign of guilt, then I don't know what it is. He has to be the Sickle Killer."

"Sickle Baby," I corrected.

"I'm not calling him that."

"You really think so?" Adjutant Ji Ping said, looking up from the stack of paperwork on his desk.

"Isn't it obvious? He knew all the details of how the Sickle Killer murdered—even the flowers in the mouth."

"Sickle Baby," I corrected again.

"Then why would he hang around the crime scene?" Ji Ping said, ignoring me.

"Maybe he got spooked. We were going to catch him."

"He only got spooked because you think he's the one that's behind it all," Ji Ping said with some irritation.

"That's because he *is* behind it all," Captain Chen bit back.

I stared up at the ceiling beams. The red lacquer was peeling. Thin flicks of it threatened to drift down onto my desk. Even though we put in a request for the beams to be painted again, no one had fixed it yet[4]. I mean, what does it take to get a simple request like that taken care of? An order from the governor?

Maybe I should see if he can get someone moving on this.

And then I remembered that I was currently on the governor's bad list.

Sure, there was paperwork I needed to do, but I wasn't going to do it today. And before you ask, I wasn't depressed. I was just…a little dispirited, that's all. Staring up at the ceiling beams seemed far more interesting than reading documents and stamping forms. That was what Ji Ping was for.

Ji Ping and Captain Chen continued to argue while Officer Ruo occasionally interjected. I didn't think Captain Chen was right. There was genuine worry in the storyteller's voice and a genuine softness to Tian Mei's mannerism when she talked to him. She had a tender side, even if she only showed it to a handful of people.

"Then what about the Jade Beauty?" Ji Ping asked.

"What about her?" Captain Chen asked.

"She could have killed them both." Ji Ping said. "She had lots of reasons to kill Peng Ning and Ding Enlai."

"She had motive, but she didn't know the case."

"Does it matter? We've seen her temper. She could have learned the details of the Sickle Killer's behavior and then copied it to send a message."

"Don't talk about her like that," Officer Ruo interjected. "She's innocent."

"What makes you say that?"

"Well…she…"

"You're going to say that she's innocent because she's beautiful, aren't you?" Ji Ping accused.

"That's not what I'm trying to say," Officer Ruo said.

"Beautiful people are just as capable of murder as ugly people," Ji Ping said with a sneer.

"She doesn't fit the profile," Officer Ruo said. "She's not the kind of person that would remove someone's hands."

For a moment, we all stared at Ruo in surprise. And then, almost as one, we burst out into laughter.

He glared at us. "What's so funny?"

"I didn't think you had it in you!" Captain Chen chuckled. "Look at you sounding like a real investigator."

"I am a real investigator!"

"You're always swooning over her. We didn't think you'd be able to see past that," Ji Ping added.

"It's true," I said with a grin. "You're a sucker for a pretty face."

"I can't believe you guys. I am sworn to uphold the law!" Officer Ruo huffed. "I am an officer of the Tribunal!"

We burst out laughing again.

"He's cute when he's offended, isn't he?"

"You guys are the worst. It's no wonder I'm so traumatized from working here. Every day is horror," Officer

Ruo said in his best impersonation of a stage actor. He had a good life. We were good co-workers. There was no way he was actually traumatized. "I don't know why I keep coming back here."

"You're too stupid to know better!"

Trauma.

A sudden thought came to my mind and the accompanying urge to groan loudly at something I missed. Tang Luli, the Jade Beauty's *baomu*, had once seen the Sickle Killer murder her friend, and was almost killed by him herself. At first, I thought it impossible that she would want to relive that trauma, but could she be murdering people in the same way because she was trapped in her memory?

If I were the Jade Beauty, would I want someone to rescue me? That didn't feel right. I remembered how she kept insisting to Tang Luli and Mao Gang that she could protect herself. That meant that there was a disconnect between her and whoever was killing for her.

Was it possible…?

"I *know* it's not the Jade Beauty," Officer Ruo said. "In fact, I'm willing to put up some money on it."

"Oh-ho!" Captain Chen said. "I'll take that bet. Are you getting in on this, Magistrate? Ji Ping?"

Ji Ping shook his head. "I don't make stupid bets."

"You think you're better than us?" Captain Chen teased.

"I *know* I'm better than you."

"I'll take that bet," I said with a grin. I knew he was probably right, but I didn't care. My men liked it when I joined them in this sort of 'stupid bet.'

The door to the office slid open with a loud and sudden thunk and a clerk came running into the office. I recognized him as the one that informed us of Peng Ning's murder. That felt like a lifetime ago.

"Magistrate!" he blurted out as he ran towards my desk. "Magistrate!"

"What is it?" I said, sitting upright. "Another murder?"

"No..." he stammered. "Something else."

"Never mind then." I slumped back into my seat.

"I brought you a message. A young man handed me this note and said I needed to deliver it to you immediately."

"Who was it from?" Ji Ping said, snatching the note out of the clerk's hands.

"He didn't say," the clerk said.

"Thank you," Ji Ping said with a dismissive wave of his hand.

I fought a smile. Sure, I'm in charge around here, but let's be real: Ji Ping's in charge here[5]. My adjutant handed me the note. I unfolded the paper. A thin looking script that was a little on the messy side, the writing had its own unique flair to it. It wouldn't have passed any calligrapher's critique, but it was legible, at least.

"What does it say, Magistrate?" Captain Chen said.

Right. I needed to read the note and not look at the handwriting.

Magistrate,

I'm sorry. By now you must have figured out that I stole the sickles from the Tribunal. But I didn't kill anyone. Everything has gone wrong. Meet me by the alley across from the Golden Ingot this evening. I'll explain everything.

Mao Gang

"Did you really figure out that it was Mao Gang that stole the sickles?" Captain Chen asked.

"Of course," I lied with a boisterous laugh. "What do you take me for?"

My squad exchanged a skeptical look.

I really hate them sometimes.

"So he says it's not him. Are we going to arrest him anyway?"

"It's not our case anymore, remember?" Ji Ping said, shaking his head.

"But I guess I should meet him anyway—see what he has to say," I said.

"Alone?" Ji Ping asked skeptically.

"Maybe," I shrugged.

"Absolutely not," Ji Ping said.

"Magistrate, at least let me go with you," Captain Chen said.

"He's going to kill you if you go alone," Officer Ruo warned.

I grabbed Joy from behind my desk and shook it at them. "I know a thing or two, you know. I'm not a useless idiot like some other magistrates around here."

"At least take Ji Ping with you," Captain Chen said.

"He can't help you in a fight," Officer Ruo said. "I should go with you."

"You're too conspicuous," Ji Ping said.

I sighed. "Fine, Ji Ping, you're coming with me."

I don't know why Ji Ping smirked, but I ignored it.

"We'll meet him and see what he has to say. Who knows?" I shrugged. "Maybe we'll get lucky."

WE DID NOT GET LUCKY.

In fact, we were very unlucky.

Given my luck lately, I suppose I shouldn't have been surprised that he'd be dead by the time we arrived. In all the stories, whenever someone says 'I have something to tell you, meet me at the super special spot,' they usually end up dead. It's like a self-fulfilling curse of sorts.

As far as alleyways went, this was probably one of the cleaner ones in the city. Between the refuse of the discarded crates, food detritus, and other unmentionables, Mao Gang's body lay in the middle of a small clearing in the alleyway across from the Golden Ingot. He lay front down on the ground, his face turned to the side. There was something of a look of horror on his face. Blood splattered around his body.

I touched the flesh of his skin. Still warm. He couldn't have been dead for long. I looked around. On one side, the alley led to the main thoroughfare of the Long'cheng district. On the other side, the alley extended further down into what I knew was to be a mess of alleys and back streets.

Unlike the other crime scenes, there was no mutilation of

the body. His hands were still intact, and I could only make out the wounds of a confrontation.

"A deep slash in the back, made by a curved blade," I said, examining the body.

"He must have tried to run."

"But this didn't kill him…" I gingerly lifted his head. "A slit throat as well. Our best lead is dead."

"It's not our case anymore, Magistrate," Ji Ping reminded me. The old nag. I swear, he's worse than my wife.

"I've lost my only fan," I said, remembering how earnest he was when he said he admired my work. I wasn't comfortable with having a fan before, but now losing him? He's gone and now no one liked me[1] anymore.

"We have no idea what he wanted to tell you," Ji Ping said, ignoring my sentiment.

"Check his body. Maybe he's carrying something."

"Me?" Ji Ping wrinkled his nose. "This is the sort of thing for Chen or Ruo."

"Well, they're not here."

Ji Ping knelt down beside me with a grumble and patted down Mao Gang's body. A slight crunch came from inside his robe. Wincing, he leaned over his body to fish out a scroll. He handed the scroll to me. In the dim light from the main road, I read the note.

My own writing—somehow the kid got a hold of it:

"There's some evidence that he may have worked with an accomplice—someone less powerful than him that helped him find his victims. I can't confirm it, and he was not forthcoming in revealing their identity, no matter how much force was applied during interrogation."

The storyteller was onto the same thought that I was, only I thought that Mao Gang could have been the accomplice.

"A master and an apprentice," I said out loud as I rose.

"What was that?" Ji Ping asked, straightening.

"During the first Sickle Killer case, I thought there could

have been an apprentice that helped the Sickle Killer. We never found any evidence to prove or disprove it, though."

"Could the Jade Beauty be the apprentice?" Ji Ping asked. "Maybe she was his apprentice when he was still killing."

"She would have been eight years old? It's possible."

"Could she have killed Mao Gang?"

"Perhaps with the murder of Peng Ning and Ding Enlai, but not this one." I shook my head.

"You mean Officer Ruo is right?"

"Sort of. This doesn't fit the profile. There's no enjoyment here—just a death. We don't even know if it's the same killer."

Check the mouth for a Chrysanthemum flower, I remembered Mao Gang saying. Another one of those obscure details of the case that most laymen wouldn't have known. I leaned over his head, placed one hand on his chin and another clamping the sides of his cheeks for leverage. Gently, I tugged his jaw down.

"You were right, Mao Gang," I sighed.

"We should do something about this," he said.

"We can't." I shook my head. "We're off the case, remember?"

"It doesn't seem right to leave him here."

"You have some discreet ways of letting the Tribunal know about this, don't you?"

"I suppose…"

"Then let's do a sweep of the scene—make our own notes of what happened. We'll figure this out on our own and swoop in and claim all the glory. But before that…"

"What is it?"

"I don't think we're alone," I whispered. I made a slight nod upwards. "When I give the signal, run to the main road."

Ji Ping stiffened, but nodded. I unsheathed Joy as quietly as possible.

"Go!" I yelled. Ji Ping ran.

The attack came from above. First, were three throwing knives aimed at Ji Ping's retreating form that I deflected with my blade. He made it to the end of the alleyway, and then the Sickle Baby was on me, and I couldn't keep track of him any longer.

"We've got to stop meeting like this!" I said.

I couldn't get a read of them because of the mask they wore. Fighting someone with two weapons is tricky business at best. Fighting them in an alleyway with refuse, night soil, blood, and a dead body at your feet? Even trickier.

But I eat tricks for breakfast. [2]

Ok, I know that catchphrase doesn't work[3]. Let's just get on with it.

"What, no witty banter? That's what makes these fights fun!"

I parried a combination of three slashes from their sickles and then closed the distance between us. I struck out with my palm, hitting them in the chest with *Mufei's Palm Strike*. They let out a high-pitched grunt and retreated three steps before they launched themselves into another attack. They moved with snakelike speed, and it was all I could do to avoid their strikes.

I need to end this.

"Did you really need to kill Mao Gang? He wasn't ever going to hurt Tian Mei, and you know it," I said, retreating a few steps. I circled them as best I could in a narrow alleyway. "You made a mistake."

They didn't answer, but I felt them tense at the Jade Beauty's name.

I channeled my qi, felt the familiar tingling through my limbs passing through my hands and into Joy.

Echo of the Blue Mountain!

Echo was the signature move of the Sword of the Nine Dragons—the style taught at Blue Mountain. When *Echo* combined with the swords Sorrow or Joy, it became an unblockable technique. Joy sliced through both sickles, and their blades clattered uselessly to the ground. Sickle Baby recovered quicker than I expected, and my follow-up strike clipped them on the right arm above the elbow.

They grunted in pain, retreated five steps, then kicked a ruined crate towards my face. I'm not going to tell you that I got hit by a piece of wood or that it stunned me momentarily. Instead, I'll tell you I was able to heroically avoid it. The crate was the distraction they needed. With a qinggong assisted leap, they scaled the wall and up onto the roof of the nearby building.

"We'll see each other soon," I said to the night.

With the coast clear, Ji Ping returned to my side. Ji Ping was not a fighter, and even though he could be extraordinarily brave, I never liked it when he was nearby in a fight. I checked him for wounds, and when I found that he was unharmed, I let out a sigh of relief.

"Maybe we should have brought Ruo along."

"Do you hear that?" he asked suddenly, craning his head down the alleyway.

A low moan.

"If you're here, come out," I said loudly. "We're not going to hurt you."

"We just want to ask you a few questions about the murder here. If you need aid, we'll take you to a doctor," Ji Ping called out. "This is Magistrate Tao Jun. We're here to assist."

"Heeeelp," someone moaned.

About five bu^4 down the alleyway, an old man lay atop a heap of discarded fabric behind some crates. It was as makeshift of a bed as you could get, and I was honestly kind of surprised to see this sort of thing in the Long'cheng district. A homeless man living on the streets of the district was simply something that the nobles would not have tolerated.

His eyes looked wild, and they darted between Ji Ping and me, like a trapped animal. Beyond his unkempt appearance and his scraggly beard, he wore little more than rags, dirt-stained and soiled. The smell was unbelievable. It was a foul concoction of back alley and body odor mixed with the contents of a *matong*[5].

"Easy there, we're not here to hurt you," I said.

Ji Ping knelt at the man's side, checking his wounds. There was a nick across his cheek and one on his arm. They didn't look serious at all, but the old man was clearly shaken.

"What happened to you?" I asked.

"She's going to kill me!"

"The one with the mask?"

He didn't answer.

"Who was it?"

He shook his head.

"Was it a beautiful woman?"

"I couldn't make out her face...she was...violent. Killed the young man. She put on the mask when she saw me. I told her I didn't see anything and then tried to run."

"So it was a woman," Ji Ping said, shaking his head. "The Jade Beauty."

"We don't know that, Ji Ping."

"She cut me! *Lao tian*, I'm going to bleed to death," the homeless man cried.

"It's just a scratch," I said, checking his wounds again.

"I'm bleeding everywhere!"

"You're barely bleeding. I've had skinned knees worse than this," I said, rolling my eyes. "Did you see anything that you can tell us?"

He shook his head.

"Really?" I said, in a disbelieving tone. "You saw nothing?

That's too bad, because we were going to take you to the doctor…"

"No, please! You have to help me!"

"Hmmm, you know I actually forgot where the closest doctor is around here…"

"Wait, I remember something…they were arguing!" he said triumphantly.

When he didn't continue, I added, "That's it?"

"Yes?"

"What were they arguing about?" I said through clenched teeth.

"I'm dying—I can't remember!"

"Hmmm, I don't remember how to treat these wounds either," I said with a shrug. Ji Ping frowned in disapproval. The old nag.

"No, wait! I remember them arguing about someone, and then the woman said something about 'never touch anyone again,' and then…blood!"

"And where were you during this whole time?"

"I had just come out of my home to see what was going on. I thought the lady needed help, but then she cut me! Oh, my arm!"

"If she wanted you dead, you would be dead."

"She was going to kill me, I'm sure of it! But when she heard you both coming up the alley, she went up on the roof."

"All right, let's get him to a doctor," I added. "Can you stand, old man?"

"I'm not old," he shook his head. "I'm twenty-five."

My jaw dropped, and I caught another whiff of his stench. I felt my dinner rise and the urge to gag.

"Ji Ping, you take him to the doctor. Find out what else he knows," I said, pinching my nose.

I didn't expect much else, but something finally made sense. Maybe part of it was the process of elimination. But I finally knew who the Sickle Killer was.

"Where are you going?"

"Home. I have an idea."

"What? I have to keep working and you get the rest of the night off?"

"Send me a report in the morning!" I said, waving. "You're the best!"

17

Before going home, I needed to see Lao Wang. Most of the bustle of the evening had died down as people returned to their homes. The adrenaline from my earlier fight with the Sickle Baby had long burned out, and I could feel fatigue start to enter my limbs.

Nevertheless, Lao Wang and I needed to chat first. It was a quiet night in his garden. The last blossoms of the season gathered by his feet, and a stillness rested in his garden like the pause before a great sigh.

"Hello, old friend," I said, sitting next to him. "I have something difficult to do, and I wanted to speak with you first."

He greeted me with silence, beckoning me to continue.

"The Sickle Baby is not the Sickle Killer. The Jade Beauty is at the heart of this all—she's the key—which means she could be in serious danger if I make a move."

I felt the loss of Mao Gang more keenly than the other victims of the Sickle Baby. I regretted all the suspicion I heaped on him, the distrust. Sure, he was an accomplice, but he was earnest enough and tried to make amends in the end. I wondered how he would have spun this part of the story. *Our brave and handsome hero, Magistrate Tao Jun, sought out the wisdom of his old friend. He sat beside his stone companion and...*

And what?

Muttered heroically? Is that possible?

Looking back on it now, I don't know if pursuing the case after the governor's efforts to shut it down was the right decision. Maybe my own professional pride was still getting in the way, but I knew I had to catch this killer—if only to bring a killer to justice.

His silence was damning and encouraging.

"Remember how they call me the Magistrate of the Torch? It's not the most flattering nickname, I know. But there's a good reason for it. I got that name because I ordered the extermination of an entire village. It wasn't my proudest moment, but it's one that has come to define me. I'm not the Magistrate of the Torch because of the licks of flame that consumed the village and its inhabitants.

"I wear that name with pride because it's a reminder. When it comes down to it, I won't hesitate to make the tough call—even if it means that justice punishes the innocent. I've seen others suffer from the consequences of my decisions. But I've also seen justice fall on those that otherwise wouldn't have received it because of my actions."

We sat in silence for a few moments.

There's a look in the eyes of wartime doctors that I can feel deep in my bones. I remember seeing it in the surgeons on the front after a long shift, and they can't count the number of lives they've lost and saved. They make the tough call. Sometimes, to save a life, they take a limb. Sometimes, to save a life, they have to let another die. And maybe that life saved would rather have died than be maimed. It's not a great choice, but it's a necessary one.

It's a choice that people count on me to make.

"Lao Wang, I don't seek out these choices. The gods in their heavens above know that I never want to be put in that position." I leaned back on the bench and chuckled. "If I'm being honest, that's why I feign ignorance or incompetence. If you're an idiot, they're not going to force you to make that choice." I sighed.

Unfortunately, the magistrate's seal I carry says otherwise.

"For some reason, people think I'm competent enough to make these decisions. How in all of the bureaucrats of hell would they know? Thanks to that seal, even if I make a mistake, no one is going to tell me to my face. They're too scared that I'll send them to prison and have them tortured."

Lao Wang reminded me of that one time where someone was walking too slowly and speaking too loudly in front of me, and I had them arrested because they were obstructing justice but really were just annoying me.

"Anyway, that was not my fault.[1]" I reassured him, though I knew he didn't believe me. "The sick and twisted thing about life is that in order to reward you for making tough decisions, they stick you back into that hellhole and force you to make more tough decisions. Your reward is punishment.

"The thing about hard choices is this: if no one else will make them, you have to do it. Because if you want justice, sometimes you have to take it for yourself. I'm sure you know this, Lao Wang, but the gods in all their capricious nature will not intervene and save us. We have to save ourselves and mete out justice where we can."

"Well, obviously. What are you going to do about it?" Lao Wang seemed to say. He can be so wise sometimes.

I rose from my seat and turned to leave the garden. I felt the lingering grasp of my doubts, the irrationality that threatened to take over even as I chose otherwise.

"Lao Wang, I've got to stop doubting myself. I'm going to make it right. I'm going to catch the Sickle Baby in the only way I know how. And if it means endangering someone like the Jade Beauty? You can bet I'll do it."

18

WHEN I ARRIVED HOME THAT NIGHT, I ASKED THE SERVANTS TO find my wife and bring her to my study. Shao Lan wasn't used to being summoned in this way, and she made her displeasure known from the moment she entered. Her face bore the darkness and fury of a summer storm, and I knew if I let her start, I'd be hit by lightning.

"I have good news for you," I said, smiling my most charismatic, charming smile.

"That's hard to believe," she said, crossing her arms skeptically.

"I've given some thought to the marriage stuff you wanted," I said solemnly.

"Oh?" She perked up.

"I want you to invite Tian Mei over for tea tomorrow morning. I want to get a move on this…marriage business."

She looked stunned for a moment, and then her shock turned into a smile, which caused me a pang of guilt. I was lying to her. "You've made a decision?"

"I want to see what she's like…you know, when I'm not investigating her for murder," I said. I suppose I should have said something for my real purpose of inviting her over, but I didn't. Shao Lan would never have agreed.

"I still can't believe you investigated her." She clicked her tongue in annoyance.

"You can't blame me for that. She was a murder suspect."

"You should apologize to her."

"I'm not apologizing to her for doing my job."

"You will if you know what's good for you."

"I'm sorry that I was harsh with you through the investigation," I apologized. I offered a short bow to Tian Mei. I could feel the smirk of satisfaction radiating from my wife. I tried my best to ignore it, but it was like ignoring the sun on a clear day. "You must understand—it's part of the job."

"Compared to that *bendan*, Magistrate Ku, you were like the goddess of mercy. I accept your apology." She sniffed with the faintest hint of an imperious glare. She then turned to my wife and beamed at her with a glorious smile like the first light of morning. "Shao Lan, how wonderful it is to see you again."

"Dear Tian Mei," my wife said, embracing her. "I've missed you so."

"You wouldn't believe the nightmare I've lived through the last few weeks." She pouted in her hug. "It was horrible."

"You're such a dear for enduring it so well."

I shouldn't have been surprised by her change in behavior, but I was. I expected her to be hostile, a bundle of glares and spite, but in front of Shao Lan, Tian Mei was actually kind of pleasant.

"At least she's safe and clear of blame," Tang Luli said at Tian Mei's side. She bowed to Shao Lan and then presented her with a small box. "A little gift from the Luminous Moon, my Lady Shao."

She used her left hand.

"Lady Tang," my wife bowed, then embraced the older woman. They looked to be around the same age. I was surprised. I didn't expect them to know each other.

"Sister," Tang Luli said in greeting.

Sister? When did that happen? I fought the urge to groan. There was no possible solution to this case that didn't involve someone getting hurt.

But I had to push it forward.

You understand, right?

"It's too bad someone couldn't find that nasty murderer," Shao Lan said. She didn't have to look at me, but I could feel the condescension pouring off in waves like rainwater in a monsoon.

I fought the urge to scowl. I was supposed to be on my best behavior. I don't understand why everyone always wants me to be on my best behavior. I don't do best behavior. Everyone should know this by now. I just do me. My behavior. If I'm charming, I'm charming. If it's rude, it's rude. I don't need to change anything. I am what I am.[1]

"The governor intervened, fortunately," Tang Luli said. "Lady Tian Mei should be above reproach."

"She's not above the law," I gently reminded.

The wife shot me a dark look.

"It's true," I muttered. "No one is above the law."

And all of this political interference is exactly why I hate my job.

Sure, there was the framework of the law, and in theory, it was supposed to protect everyone. We're supposed to enforce it, maintain it, and in return, we'd reap the rewards of peace. In reality, the rules of the law were flaunted and often outright broken by those who had power. And in cases like this, where a high-profile member of society came up against the law, we saw exactly how effective the law was.

I shook my head.

It wasn't the first time the governor intervened in a case. It certainly wouldn't be the last. Justice? Please, you sound so naïve. If they were willing to play fast and loose with the law, then I certainly was willing to as well.

I had a murderer to catch, after all.

"I'm just glad you're safe," my wife said, embracing Tian Mei again. "That murderer could have killed you."

"She was never in any danger," Tang Luli said.

What an odd thing to say, I thought.

"What makes you say that?" my wife asked.

"Because, she was clearly the victim here. All of those men preying on her, and someone is protecting her," the *baomu* said with a sniff. "As far as I'm concerned, the Sickle Killer is a hero."

"That's an interesting perspective," I said. "I haven't heard many killers described as heroes before."

"Oh, but her safety is all that matters," the *baomu* said hurriedly.

A look of annoyance flashed across the Jade Beauty's face.

"I can take care of myself," she said. "They're not after me."

"Not anymore," the *baomu* said. "The killer certainly put an end to those men."

"Tang Luli, you shouldn't say things like that," Tian Mei chided. "This is the magistrate's home. I wouldn't want him to arrest you for saying such outlandish things."

"The governor shut down the case. I'm not here to investigate anyone. I'm just here to have tea." I smiled at them in the most pleasant way I knew how.

I act like a fool a lot, and there are a couple of reasons for that. The first is a matter of laziness. If people think that you're a fool, then they don't give you as much to do. Unless they see right through all that, in which case you're stuck.

The second reason is that it's the perfect disguise. If you're a fool, people underestimate you. They get sloppy, and they don't have their guard up. When they think you're a fool, people get careless—like being careless at what they say in front of me. Expressing sympathy for a murderer is something that I hear a lot, funny enough.

But it's little crumbs like that, that can break a mystery right open.

"Why don't you show Tian Mei the gardens? I want to have a little chat with Lady Tang." My wife beamed at me, looking very pleased. She linked arms with Tang Luli, taking her by the elbow. She thinks she's so smart, leaving us in the garden alone. As though I can't see right through her attempts to make me spend time with the Jade Beauty.

"I would love to," I replied, noting the way the *baomu* winced from Shao Lan's touch. There was a flicker of worry on Tang Luli's face, but she quickly hid it behind a smile. I could sense the *baomu's* disapproval, though I suspected that she would have disapproved of any man. Still, I kind of bristled at that. I was a noble and a magistrate. I would be a great catch for any dozen women.

"Lady Tian Mei," I said, bowing. "Would you please follow me?"

She gave a polite nod, and I led her into the garden.

All things considered, it was a beautiful day. Spring birds chirped in the mid-morning, singing their song of life. The weather wasn't too hot or cold, and the sun shone down with the kind of brilliance that was perfect for a romantic stroll through the garden.

I like romance, but today it was about justice.[2]

I led her along the main path through the garden, across the stone bridge, and towards the pavilion by the koi pond.

"I'm sorry for the rough start to our relationship," I said, breaking the silence between us. "A criminal investigation is not the best way to begin."

She gave me a rueful smile. "I heard you were taken off the case."

"Despite the governor's insistence on burying it, I still have some ideas."

"Oh?" She turned to me and flashed a brilliant smile, and for a moment I saw why she was the desire of the martial world. "You still don't think it's me, do you?"

"Maybe."

I reached out and took her by the right arm.

"What are you doing?"

"Checking something," I squeezed her arm above the elbow, feeling the muscle beneath the soft silk of her dress. She didn't flinch or wince but gave me a curious look instead. No trace of blood.

Finally, I knew it couldn't be her.

"I hurt the Sickle Baby when I fought them," I said. "Cut them in the arm. It's not you."

"I could have told you that," she sighed. "Sickle Baby?" she said with some skepticism.

Everyone's a critic.

"I needed to make sure," I tried to make a joke. "Can't exactly marry a serial killer."

She offered a thin smile. "You really want that?"

"It's what Shao Lan wants," I said with a shrug.

"And what she wants, she gets?"

"Something like that."

"That bodes well for me too, if we marry." She giggled, and I was completely thrown off by the change in her attitude. Who was this woman, and where did the young lady that I watched destroy Peng Ning and Ding Enlai go?

"Is that something you want?"

She shrugged. "There are worse people to be married to."

"Gee thanks," I frowned.

"You could be bald or smell of fish." She smiled again. "At least here I can be with Shao Lan. She's wonderful."

"Not smelling like fish is a pretty low bar to clear."

"And one that is surprisingly hard for some men."

I wondered what kind of history this young woman could have had with my wife but pushed the thought away. I had a job to do.

The moment of mirth was as brief as it was sudden. She sobered immediately. "To tell you the truth, the whole matter bothers me deeply."

"You're at the center of it."

She nodded.

"Whoever it is, is killing people they think are a threat to me."

"So you've noticed. Do you have any idea who it is? Any suspicions?"

"I…" she stammered. "It was Mao Gang. It's a shame that it was."

I arched an eyebrow. "Why do you think that is?"

She frowned and shook her head. "I can't say."

"You two were close, weren't you? He used to protect you when you were both orphans," I said quietly.

She jerked to a stop, her face growing pale. "How did you know that?"

I didn't answer her and instead leaned on the balustrade of the pavilion. A koi swam up to the surface, snapped up a water strider, and then swam back into brown depths.

"He hadn't seen you in a while, but instead of a happy reunion, he found you harassed by Peng Ning and Ding Enlai. And then they humiliated you."

"I showed them what I thought of that."

"You did. And then they ended up dead."

"He…must have killed them," she sighed. "It makes sense. Years ago, when we were children, he was always one to try to protect me. He got in so many fights because of that."

I held her gaze, saying nothing.

"It makes sense, doesn't it, Magistrate? It was him," she said, looking at me. "He's the type of person that is ultra-protective and possessive and then becomes unhinged over time," she said smugly. "Since this whole ordeal started, I started to learn a bit about criminals. It sounds like him. Isn't it what you say—it fits the profile?"

I fought the urge to roll my eyes. These kids learn a few things about reading people and suddenly they think they know something about criminals. "There's a bit more to it than that."

"Ha. I'm sure."

"Does he really fit that? Was he becoming unhinged at the end?"

She frowned. "Maybe he was more protective the more worried he got. I don't know about unhinged."

"Why weren't you this forthcoming with me during the investigation? It would have made things easier."

"I was…under a lot of pressure. I couldn't trust you."

"And now? You suddenly trust me?"

"Well, you're not investigating me," she said. Then her cheeks flushed slightly. "And you might be my future husband."

Well, that was a terrifying thought. As beautiful as she was, the thought of sharing a home with a woman with a temperament even more unpredictable than Shao Lan was enough to send me running. *Maybe I could rebuild Blue Mountain and live there. I'll be a recluse for the rest of my days and live in utter peaceful bliss.*

"I didn't know if you were like Magistrate Ku—only interested in their own career and not the truth. So many of the men I meet are like that."

"I am nothing like Magistrate Ku," I said with maybe a little bit more heat than intended because she seemed taken aback. I bowed my head in a simple apology and changed the topic. "Have you seen Mao Gang lately?"

Her earlier suspicion returned for a moment as she considered whether I was going to arrest him; then she shook her head. "We had a disagreement at the Red Peony after Ding Enlai was killed. He left and went into hiding. I told him he needed to run since you were all looking for him. I'm sure he's far away from here by now. I just hope he won't kill anyone again."

She leaned on the pavilion's balustrade, watching the koi swim in the pond below. Her expression softened, and there was such a lovely wistful quality to her face that I hesitated.

I took a deep breath.

"Mao Gang is dead."

"What?" The wistful smile slowly dropped and was replaced by the angry knitting of her eyebrows. "If this is a joke..."

"It's not. I saw his body yesterday," I said quietly. "I'm sorry."

"He's gone?" She turned away from me to look back at the pond, and I saw that her eyes glistened with tears.

"But then..." she gathered herself quickly. "But then, who is it?"

"That's what I've been thinking about for a while. Magistrate Ku thought it was you, and for a long time, all the proof pointed your way. But that solution didn't sit right with me. You see, Magistrate Ku didn't witness the tenderness between you and Mao Gang. There was no way you'd kill him like this."

She blinked away tears.

"And you're a far more direct person than the Sickle Baby. An Almighty Slap? That's your style. Not dismemberment. There's only one other person that it could be," I said. "It's someone close to you."

"What?" Her hand rose to her mouth in shock.

She really didn't know? And from the sincerity in her eyes, I knew that I would have to spell it out for her. That was a task I didn't have the heart for at this time—easier to just show her.

"You're still in danger. Like you said, they become obsessed and more and more unhinged as time goes on."

She hesitated. "I'll leave An'lin then."

"That won't work. They'll just follow you. Look, it's quiet now, but they'll be back." I shook my head. "They always come back, and the killings will begin again. And always, you will be at the heart of it."

"What should I do then?"

"Help me catch them."

She shook her head.

"The truth is that the more obsessed they become, the more likely they are to attack you as well. All it takes is some kind of rejection from you—it may not even be that dramatic, and they'll turn on you and you'll be the next victim." I sighed, leaning on the balustrade next to her. "But what do I know? It's not like I've made a career out of chasing down murderers and the lowlifes of society."

After a few moments of silence, she finally spoke up.

"What do I need to do?"

"Do you trust me?"

She nodded.

"You might not like what's coming next."

19

I STOOD CLOSE TO HER ON THE BRIDGE. I HAD A FEELING THAT WE were being watched. In fact, I was counting on it. Elsewhere, I knew Captain Chen, Ji Ping, and Officer Ruo were hiding somewhere in the garden. At my signal, they would come out and help me arrest the Sickle Baby.

At least, that was the plan. We all know how plans go.

"You really think this is going to work?" Tian Mei asked.

"I'm pretty sure it will," I said. "Make sure to sell it well."

The key was for her to pretend she was in love with me.

"Ugh," she said, rolling her eyes.

"Now, now, that's not selling it," I chided. The truth was, I didn't want to do this either.

"Oh, Tao Jun, you're so handsome!"

I winced. That was selling it a little too much.

"You'll save me from those men, won't you?"

"Of course I will!" I said, channeling my best impression of an overdramatic stage performer. "Only pledge to me that you will be mine."

I could tell that she wanted to gag.

Who was I kidding? I wanted to as well.

"I am yours, Tao Jun! Take me now or lose me forever!"

Yep, that was a little much.

In any other circumstance, and maybe with any other woman, this could have been romantic. It was certainly the right setting for it. A soft breeze moved the last of the spring's blossoms. Long tendrils of the willow tree drew long lines in the pond. The last of the spring's blossoms danced along the edges of the bridge and into the water.

I brushed a hand across her cheek, and she trembled slightly. If I didn't have to, I didn't want to kiss her. But in order for this stupid plan to work, we needed to sell it.

"My love," I said with a flourish. "Let's run away together. We'll leave all of this behind and start a new life elsewhere." If it was true romance, I probably should have whispered something like that. I pulled her in close, and she closed the rest of the distance. Her eyes shut and lips parted, waiting for the kiss. I hesitated for a moment, listening for any sounds, any signs that we were being watched by the Sickle Killer.

I leaned in for the kiss. [1]

I felt, more than heard, the approach of *baomu*.

"I'm sorry to intrude," Lady Tang said, aiming a look that was more a death threat than a glare at me. "But you need to let go of her now."

Shao Lan was a few steps behind her. She gave me an incredulous look of surprise on her face—probably from my amorous embrace of the Jade Beauty. "You really couldn't wait, could you?"

"So you've finally come," I said, still holding Tian Mei. "The Sickle Baby."

Sometimes, you make wild accusations and see what sticks. Other times, you confront them with the truth. If you're lucky, they end up being so shocked by the fact that you know, they admit to the crime.

"Don't deny it. I know it was you. I cut you on your right arm just above your elbow last night, and you've been using your left all day."

"Magistrate, I'm afraid this joke delusion of yours has gone too far," Tang Luli said with a headshake.

Sometimes wild accusations lead to surprises. Shao Lan reached over and grabbed Tang Luli's arm, squeezing tight. A small bloom of red appeared on her blue sleeve. Seeing the blood on the sleeve, Shao Lan dropped her hand and backed away, her hand rising to her mouth to cover her shock.

In my arms, Tian Mei jerked free from my grasp and stared at the woman she called *baomu*. "It was you? You're the Sickle Killer?"

"I had to do it to keep you safe. This man will not own you. No one will own you," Tang Luli said as she approached.

I tensed, waiting for a strike. I wondered what she would attack with, given that I destroyed her sickles last night.

"I don't want to have to kill you."

"Then don't. You're going to have to answer to justice," I said.

"What justice? Where is the justice for women like us?"

"You couldn't let anyone have Tian Mei. Unfortunately for you, she's going to be mine," I said, trying to provoke her.

Tian Mei's head snapped around in a glare, but I ignored it. This wasn't the time to deal with a petty thing like annoyance. She couldn't tell that I was baiting Tang Luli with my comment. I had a killer to expose, after all.

"Because that's it, isn't it? You can't let anyone else have Tian Mei," I said quietly. "You killed those men because they touched her, and you killed Mao Gang because you thought he would run away with her."

Baomu hissed. "I will die before I let anyone hurt her."

"You may not have heard this," I said slowly, "but she doesn't belong to you either."

"Yes, she does. The sect placed her in my care—she's mine!"

"For the hundredth time, I can take care of myself,

Baomu," Tian Mei said, a note of hurt creeping into the tremble of her voice.

"No, you can't," the *baomu* said, her eyes rimmed with desperation. "You need me! Yes, you need me. Without me, you'd be lost."

"Why did you kill Mao Gang? He would never have hurt me."

"He wanted to take you away from me. He wanted you to run away."

"He knew too much, didn't he?" I said. "Mao Gang sent me a note saying that he stole the weapons. He was going to explain everything to me before you killed him."

"He was too afraid to kill Peng Ning, so I did it. I took that vile man's life and made sure he wouldn't hurt anyone again. I brought justice for Lady Tian. I did it—not you or your Tribunal. I did it," she hissed. "After Ding Enlai, Mao Gang didn't want me to kill anyone anymore. He said that we were going to get caught, and I listened. But he tricked me."

"How did he trick you?"

"He wanted to run away with you." She turned her attention back to Tian Mei. "He was going to take you from me, and I couldn't have that."

"I can understand why you needed to protect her. You were a survivor of the Sickle Killer, and that was my blind spot. I didn't think you would reenact his horror on others."

"I needed to scare them, to put true fear into them so they and the others in their sects wouldn't harass her again."

And then I realized the truth. She was more than a survivor. "You were his apprentice, weren't you?"

"I was his plaything," she snapped. "He used me. I took it, so I could learn from him, and he used me over and over and over. And then when he was done, he let his friends use me." She trembled.

"I had no idea." I shuddered in sympathy. The way some men treated women...it was enough to make the blood boil.

She was a victim here—just as much as Tian Mei and the others.

"Oh no, you wouldn't, would you? I was his dirty little secret. And you and your Tribunal looked right over me, like I wasn't even there. But he taught me one important lesson—to claim justice whenever you can take it."

"You could have had a perfectly content life free from him forever," I said, shaking my head. "What a shame that you didn't take it."

"I did take it. The Luminous Palace embraced me when I had nowhere else to go."

"Then why did you kill those men?" Tian Mei asked.

"Because I love you. I only wanted to protect you from them, to save you from what happened to me. When I saw how Peng Ning and Ding Enlai and their scum would never leave you alone, I knew I was the only one that could save you. You don't know this, but they had given me their advances before. And men like that, if they couldn't have you, they'd want the next best thing. I went to them, tricking them into thinking that I would give myself to them. They let their guard down for a 'good time.'"

"By killing these people, you're not giving me the opportunity to bring them to justice," I said.

"They will never hurt anyone ever again."

"Isn't it worse for someone to rot in jail for the rest of their life?"

"They always escape punishment. Men don't protect women. Men protect men."

A part of me had to agree with her, but I couldn't let her go free. I raised a hand, and a second later, Captain Chen and Officer Ruo charged out from their hiding places to surround Tang Lulin.

"You're under arrest!" came their cry.

Tang Luli hissed, and with a flick of her wrist, two metal cylinders fell from her sleeves and into her hands. Then, with another flourish, the retractable sickle blades snapped into position. They were broken blades but still held an edge. They could still be used as weapons.

Captain Chen tossed me my sword, and I drew it in a flourish. The silver blade of Joy glittered in the light.

"You have nowhere to go. Don't try to run—you'll only make it worse for yourself."

When capturing a bad guy, you need to put on a good show. It doesn't matter if it's a lot of people watching or no one. The point of the matter is, you have to look good while doing it. Sure, some people would say that catching the bad guy is all that matters, but what are we, boring monks? Life is for living, and living is for looking good.

Plus, if you do the flourish right, your opponent might be impressed and intimidated.

Baomu took a step backwards, hesitant. But there was a look of determination in her eyes that I knew meant that we were in for a fight. And by we, I meant me, because as much as I know Captain Chen and Officer Ruo would gladly charge into battle by my side, they would be massively outmatched by Tang Luli

"I'll never let you take her!" she cried. "You're all after her!"

I didn't want to fight her. I didn't want to kill her in my own garden, in front of Tian Mei and Shao Lan. But if I had to fight her, I would.

I was about to make a sign for my men to back off and seek safety when Tian Mei strode forward and placed a hand on the *baomu's* arm, gently guiding her weapons down. With her other hand, she tugged the woman's face to hers, and rested her forehead on hers.

"*Baomu*," she said with a gentleness that I didn't know she had. "Thank you for protecting me all these years. But don't do this. Please."

"I…" the woman stammered. A cloud of desperation and

doubt covered her face, and she turned to plead with Tian Mei. "I couldn't let what happened to me happen to you as well."

"It won't—because you were there to protect me," Tian Mei said. Then she kissed the older woman on the cheek and embraced her. Tang Luli quivered for a moment in Tian Mei's embrace. Her weapons clattered to the ground, and she wept.

Her heart-rending wail echoed across the garden.

"You understand, don't you? I saw the way those men looked at you, Tian Mei. I swore that they wouldn't do the same to you."

"I would never let them. You trained me too well." Tian Mei hugged her again. "Because of you, I was never in any danger."

Then the tears fell, and even Officer Ruo behind me sniffled. I signaled for Captain Chen to arrest Tang Luli.

"Be gentle with her," I said.

Captain Chen nodded.

"I love you, *Baomu*," Tian Mei said, holding her close.

"My sweet."

20

How do these stories normally end? Unmask the true villain, celebrate the win, and watch as the heroes swagger off into the sunset? That's how the storytellers spin it, anyway. And maybe if Mao Gang were still alive, that would be how he would spin it too.

The end of this story started off well enough. After delivering Tang Luli to the custody of the Tribunal, my squad took a few moments in our office to settle some business.

"I told you all that it couldn't have been the Jade Beauty," Officer Ruo gloated. He extended a big, meaty palm. "She couldn't have done it. Now pay up."

"She could have, and you know it," Captain Chen grumbled as he fished out a handful of coins from his purse. "I can't believe this."

"You gotta stop betting like this, Chen," I chuckled. "Especially if you're going to keep seeing that girl from the Red Peony."

Captain Chen blushed furiously.

I pulled out my coin purse, dumping a handful into Officer Ruo's open hand.

"I always say you shouldn't make stupid bets," Ji Ping said with a sniff.

"Yeah, well, you weren't right either," Captain Chen sneered.

"That's why I didn't make a bet," Ji Ping said. "I'm not that dumb."

"Are you calling me stupid?"

"I don't need to if you're going to call yourself stupid."

"You—!"

"Ok, hold on. Do I have to be the mature one around here?" Officer Ruo asked, stepping between the two of them.

"It's a good thing you won," I said to Officer Ruo.

"Why's that?" His eyes narrowed in suspicion.

"You owe us all lunch, remember?"

"That's right! He vomited twice!" Captain Chen exclaimed.

"Two lunches." Ji Ping smiled smugly.

"I mean, you could make it one lunch if you took us to the Red Peony."

Officer Ruo's eyes widened. "I can't afford that kind of celebration meal. It's a week's pay to eat there."

"Sure you can!" Captain Chen grinned. "You just got paid."

"What if I gave you back your money?"

"Oh no, you're not getting out of this one," I said. "I want some chili crab *xiao longbao*."

I could have slapped *the end* there, and that would have been a fine ending. But the tales that storytellers spin and the reality of what actually happens are divergent, two sides of the same coin; mirrors in their complexity.

It was another victory, but it came at a cost.

The next morning, my wife came into my study. She slid

the door open with care and then crossed the room to where I sat. She wore a quiet sort of fury on her face, one that I had never seen before.

I'm dead.

"You used me," she said.

I rose from my desk and stood in front of her. "I suppose I should explain."

She slapped me across the face.

I deserved that one.

"You used me in your trap. You had it all planned out, and you used me!"

I nodded. "I couldn't tell you. I'm sorry."

"All I wanted was…" she trailed off, trembling with fury. Her face scrunched in a sob, a quivering rage. "Now everyone that comes to visit will worry about getting arrested. My invitation will be worth nothing. I'm a social outcast in An'lin."

I winced. I didn't think about it that way. I suppose I never thought about things from her point of view. Maybe she was just as trapped as the Jade Beauty. Maybe she was shielded from the same harassments, but was she actually free? Despite our wealth and privilege, she was just as much a prisoner of the manor as a commoner's wife—maybe even more so thanks to the norms of our society. At least a life in the *jianghu* had a measure of freedom, but here, a nobleman's wife, surrounded by servants?

This sympathy for Shao Lan was a new feeling, and after years of an indifferent marriage, I wasn't sure I liked it.

"I'm sorry. I really am. But I had to," I tried to explain. "Two nights ago, I found the body of Mao Gang, the storyteller friend of Tian Mei's, and I finally confirmed the identity of the Sickle Baby. t was then that I realized how much danger Tian Mei was in—if Tang Luli could kill someone as harmless as Mao Gang, then she was becoming unhinged," I explained.

Shao Lan appeared to calm down a bit, and the look of fury passed. For a stupid moment, I thought I was getting through to her.

She slapped me across the face again.

I suppose I deserved that one too.

"You said no one was above the law."

"Nobody is."

"What makes you any different? You're a killer too, aren't you? The only difference is you get to wave that magistrate token around and your sins are forgiven."

"I didn't kill her."

"But she's not likely going to live, is she?"

I shook my head.

It wasn't fair. As a magistrate, I've always strived for fairness. In most cases, I felt like I achieved that fairness, even at the expense of the law. Shao Lan's words cut me deep, and she brought out the nagging truth of the Sickle Baby's spree of murder. In this, nobody won. A woman, driven to madness from the horror of her youth, set out to protect the one she loved against the men that would ruin her. She mete out her own form of justice, only to find death waiting for her in the end.

"All I wanted was a companion in this house. Someone that would accompany me, and listen to me, and be my friend. It was a simple request. But in the end, what I want is still swallowed up by what you want," she said bitterly. "Magistrate Tao Jun, the hero of An'lin."

"Shao Lan," I said quietly. "I'm sorry."

She walked away, leaving me alone with my thoughts.

The hero of An'lin. Shao Lan's words haunted me, leading me to introspection I didn't normally feel. I suppose her reaction should have been a warning sign to me—a prophecy of sorts for everything else that happened after. In public, the governor was thrilled that I was able to capture the Sickle Baby and bring her to justice. He rewarded me in front of the court, made a big speech, and praised me for my diligence.

In private, he was furious that I went up against his effort to bury the case. There wasn't even a hint of gratitude. He yelled at me and proceeded to go through all of my shortcomings. He didn't use to care about this sort of thing. Something had him on edge and extra sensitive, and I wondered if it had something to do with the Black Tiger Rebellion. Or maybe it was because two of the biggest martial sects in the area were suddenly without proper leadership, and given the state of their affairs, were likely to break into open conflict with one another.

Either way, I didn't understand his change in attitude—and I still don't.

Even days after Tang Luli's arrest, I couldn't stop thinking about her. What set her off to start murdering people? Surely she must have witnessed harassment of Tian Mei before—what made the summit any different? In many cases, things started to make sense towards the close, but here I only found more questions[1]. I wasn't going to be getting my answers either—the governor ruled that no one could talk to Tang Luli.

A cover-up of a series of murders and two of the most prominent sects in the area without leaders—I couldn't help but feel that there was something bigger going on here.

I sought out the Jade Beauty to apologize. After talking to Shao Lan, I realized how destructive my actions were, even if I had captured a killer. Capturing the bad guy makes you a hero, right? But I certainly didn't feel like one.

I arrived at the headquarters of the Luminous Moon Palace. A beautiful estate on the eastern side of the Long'cheng district, it was a place that could rival the governor's own residence. At least that's what the rumors said. I didn't make it in through the main gate.

The servants at the door recognized me immediately but refused to let me in. True to their secretive form, they even kept the mundane things, like what the inside of their headquarters looked like, a mystery.

"I'm sorry, Your Excellency, we do not permit any outsiders inside."

"I'm here to see Lady Tian Mei—official business," I fished out my seal from where it dangled at my waist and held it up for them to see.

They weren't impressed.

"Lady Tian Mei is indisposed at this time," the servant said.

I frowned. "What's wrong? Is she unwell?"

"I'm not at liberty to say."

That can't be good.

"I need to see Lady Tian Mei," I repeated.

"We will tell her you came by," they said, bowing.

I knew a dismissal when I saw one. For a moment I thought about making a bigger stink about it, but then again I was already on the governor's bad side today, and it would only make things worse. Puzzled, I left.

It was oddly still when I returned to the manor. I came home in the early evening at the end of a particularly long day. I thought the servants would be preparing an evening meal, but the normal bustle of activity sounded muted. I wandered the halls of my home. The bustle of servants had slowed to the patter of occasional footsteps. When I passed, they spoke in low whispers.

Something had happened.

I found our household steward trembling outside of my

study. Sweat glistened off his forehead in the golden glow coming from the hallway window. He bowed immediately when he saw me.

"What's going on?" I asked him.

"Excellency, the lady—"

My eyes narrowed. "Lady Shao Lan?"

"She…" he stammered. "She left this for me to give you."

He handed over a scroll. I opened it, a grave anxiety rising in my gut.

There was only one column of words:

I have left with Tian Mei. We are going to make a life together. Don't follow us.

"Excellency, are you okay?" the steward's voice came as though he was far away.

"I guess I don't have a wife anymore." I chuckled, a little relieved, a little nervous, a little afraid. "And here I almost had two wives."

MAGISTRATE TAO JUN'S STORY WILL CONTINUE

NOTES

Chapter 1

1. Everyone that says so also receives a paycheck from Tao Jun, so....
2. *Hundan* is a jerk or a bastard. It's not a very nice thing to call someone.
3. *Jianghu* literally means rivers and lakes, but it's also the catchall term for the martial arts world and its surrounding community. Also known as "the scene," or the underworld. A loose culture of itinerant martial artists, merchants, doctors, priests—a social space where people are away from family and home and there are very little rules. You can think of it like the frontier or the wild west.
4. *Laoban* - a proprietor or boss. It's not an archaic term either. You can still go into a restaurant and call someone the *laoban*, and they'll be quite pleased.
5. *Wugong* - Martial arts, though this tends to lean towards the kind of martial arts that involves fighting. It's also known as gong fu or kung fu. If you watch a wuxia show, they'll more likely talk about wugong than they will kung fu. That's just how it goes in the *jianghu*.
6. *Pigu* - butt or your rear end. The thing you sit with.
7. Futou - A black hat with two oval shaped wings on either side. It was kind of like a dangly Mickey Mouse / Goofy hat before it was cool.
8. The Hero of An'lin. The Magistrate of the Torch. The Magistrate of the Golden Basket. These are just some of the nicknames that Tao Jun has collected over the years.

   Each comes with its own story that won't get told in this footnote.
9. *Jianfa* means sword technique. The fun part of this word is the construction. *Fa* means method or technique and you can put it behind just about anything. Because Jian means sword, Jian + Fa means sword technique.
10. Who were you to intervene? Just, you know, a magistrate of the city and someone that's supposed to enforce the law. That might be something he's supposed to do, but what do I know? I'm just a narrator.
11. Yan Tao of the Golden Brocade Inn (also known as the Broken Furniture Inn) used to be quite upset at how many of his guests would start fights in his establishment.

    However, he was able to turn this annoyance into a very profitable business. For his story, check out *The Duel at Broken Furniture Inn.*
12. Like *jianfa*, except with a fist. In other words, way of the fist, or fist method.

Chapter 2

1. A *bendan* is a stupid egg, which in all fairness, is what Tao Jun is.
2. In ancient Chinese mythology, the heavens and hells are full of bureaucrats are tiers of officials. Some natural disasters like floods or famines are the result of these paper pushers messing up their jobs.

    You can't escape red tape - even in mythology.
3. In all fairness, to anyone else, it probably was a sweet smile. She's just some kind of monster in his head.
4. Also, in all fairness, they probably didn't respect him *that* much.

Chapter 3

1. *Goupi* is a dog fart. It's like calling BS on someone.
2. Actually, the worst liar he ever met once tried to sell him a goat, claiming that if you rubbed your head on its...you know...you'd get more...performance.

    Needless to say, our hero saw right through that one too.
3. See the *Touch of Murder, The Tale of the Magistrate, Vol. 1*.
4. Ji Ping would say that Tao Jun's job is to sign and affix his seal to the proper documents, but when has Tao Jun ever taken that part of his job seriously.

    Answer: never.
5. Not a polite word to use. It's kind of like SOB as an expletive.
6. It definitely wasn't because he didn't trust them with the scrolls. Nope.

Chapter 4

1. Given how gaudy Tao Jun's tastes can be, that's really saying something.
2. *Gui (gway)* - are ghosts or devils. Sometimes they're called demons.
3. A *pipa* is a stringed instrument that can be plucked or strummed. It's kind of like a lute.
4. Don't listen to him. He's super thrilled about it.
5. A storyteller spinning the *Tales of the Magistrate?* I think I like this guy.
6. This is something of a touchy subject for Tao Jun, and one that he debates his brother on all the time. What is he—a spilled bowl of congee?

Chapter 5

1. The food of the Gods. Seriously. Wow. The best translation is "soup dumpling" and that doesn't do it credit.
2. Sometimes that's from the detainee, though not all the time.
3. Hell or the underworld.

4. Sometimes Tao Jun says that there's a third half that is real, but we all know that's not how halves work, Magistrate! You can't have three halves.

Chapter 6

1. He *was* trained as a swordsman after all.
   Sometimes, you just gotta flex that.

Chapter 7

1. Not to be confused with the ultra-popular storyteller, White Tortoise. Blue Tortoise was his rival, who had a grudge so deep against White Tortoise that he went so far as to adopt a moniker he thought would mock him.
   It backfired, and made White Tortoise even more successful.
   The White Tortoise makes an appearance in *Sword of Sorrow, Blade of Joy - Tales of the Swordsman Vol. 1.*
2. He may or may not have some assassins in his back pocket. See *The Touch of Murder.*

Chapter 8

1. Lady Yue is a very powerful noble. Though her hands are 'clean,' she runs an organization that would put many criminal enterprises to shame.
   For her full story, check out *The Peacock* in *Tales of the Swordsman Vol. 1.*
2. A *biantai* is a pervert. In Japanese, that term is hentai.
3. Maybe we can make an appointment for next week, Tao Jun?

Chapter 9

1. Jin Min? The famous singer?! I must have his autograph.
2. Except the clothes he typically chooses for his disguise are way too flashy for investigative work.
3. Okay, okay. My bad. You would have fit right in.

Chapter 10

1. Good luck!
2. In other words, a perfect place to hide from his wife.
3. This is actually a reference to the famous "Beauty Trap" of the Three Kingdoms period. Diao Chan, the beautiful daughter, was asked to get in

between the 'unbreakable bond' of Prime Minister Dong Zhuo and General Lu Bu.

First promised to Lu Bu, and then to Dong Zhuo, the two men ultimately tried to kill each other over her, with Lu Bu succeeding in the end, and bringing an end to the tyrannical Prime Minister.

Chapter 11

1. Or he's just too lazy. Just saying...
2. Months of paperwork...for Ji Ping, his attendant.
3. Little did he know that a little boy watched from the window of high study. That boy observed the whole interaction and would later grow up to be ...nobody important to this or any stories.

Chapter 12

1. Tao Jun has given some thought to how he might die one day. On one of those cheery thoughts, he remembered a case he heard about where a certain poison emphasized all the delicious flavors of everything you ate right before it killed.

   He thought it would be a *delicious* way to go.

   Bad joke. I'll see myself out.
2. *Dianxue* is a form of martial arts that strikes at pressure points and meridians in the body. Often this causes paralysis or even death.
3. There was one time Ji Ping *did* like the nickname, but by that point in their relationship, he had already disapproved so many nicknames that he couldn't break precedent.

   Plus, admitting he liked it would have gone to the magistrate's head.
4. Got it. Copious.

Chapter 13

1. Closely related to that other socially unacceptable, accepted practice: gossip.
2. Magistrates Ku and Tao Jun have something of a lopsided relationship. Magistrate Ku thinks of our hero as his great nemesis—the ultimate rival in his career. He plots and schemes to find a way to one up him.

   Tao Jun just thinks the guy is an idiot and couldn't be bothered.

Chapter 14

1. Was his home really raided? Find out in *Fall of the King Saber - Tales of the Swordsman Vol. 3*.

Chapter 15

1. The fact that he has to ask is quite telling. It's obviously Ji Ping and his wife.
2. Liar. He's always hoping Magistrate Ku falls into a ditch somewhere.
3. Certainly not a Magistrate that recently began employing a secret assassin clan to do his bidding. What?
4. For the stunning saga of the ceiling beams, check out the first book. You know what, check out the third book too.
5. Oh, he finally admitted it. What is this world coming to?

Chapter 16

1. Sad trombone.
2. Silly Magistrate, tricks are for kids.
3. Catchphrases are a tricky business. You only know if they work when you try them.
4. A *bu* (步) is about 5 feet or 1.5 metres.
5. A *matong* is a chamber pot. Yum.

Chapter 17

1. It was totally his fault.

Chapter 18

1. Note: this is a terrible excuse for anyone to get away with bad behavior. If this sounds like you, you need to rethink your life.
2. He's tried this line as a hero catchphrase before. It wasn't well received.

Chapter 19

1. Whatever you do, don't start smelling like fish.

Chapter 20

1. They make sense usually because of an extensive interrogation with lots of screaming and tears.

   Was it the truth? Not always. Was it a plausible explanation? Not always either.

   Was it good enough to put on the records?

   Yep.

THE PROBLEM WITH THE JADE BEAUTY TROPE

About the Jade Beauty Trope:

A Jade Beauty is a trope that appears in some wuxia stories. Essentially, the title means that the woman is a beauty among all other beauties. On the surface? That seems fine.

But it's how these characters are portrayed that is very troubling to me. Even though women in wuxia stories can be treated as equals due to their martial skill, there are times where they are little more than a sex object or something to progress the male main character's storyline. Often, they are simply a prize to be claimed by someone (usually male).

The Jade Beauty is often a target of sexual assault by the main character. Sometimes it's 'accidental' in that there were aphrodisiacs involved or it's a case of 'mistaken identity.' Sometimes it's done with malicious intent to further the MC's own cultivation or steal the woman's power. Either way, it's not consensual and it's 100000% wrong.

Another troubling aspect of the trope is that characters in the story just treat the assault as though it was no big deal—it's barely even a footnote. The woman in question is often just 'added' to the MC's harem and is never really talked about again.

Also troubling - harem trope, but that's another rant for later.

For obvious reasons, I don't like this trope AT ALL. It's horrid and a relic of an era that we need to move away from immediately. I chose to write with this trope in mind so that I could flip it around and draw some attention to awful behavior.

Obviously, this story is just a shade of the awful stuff that happens in the real world. My female beta readers saw echoes of their own trauma in this story. They also saw echoes of their own rage at the unfairness of it all. There are many cases of women who report this kind of awful behavior and then get retaliated against.

That is so messed up. We need to do better.

A single story like mine isn't going to change anything, but if we call out bad behavior when we see it, we can change things for the better. Real change only happens when we listen to those who have been hurt or marginalized, and that will only happen when we make the effort to create safe spaces for everyone.

- JF LEE

ALSO BY JF LEE

I am building a connected world of wuxia heroes and stories. I call it the *Legends of the Martial World*. Here are some highlights!

If you're enjoying what you're reading, you can **get a free story** when you sign up for my newsletter. This light hearted spoof on martial art tropes is sure to put a smile on your face.

Duel at Broken Furniture Inn

https://dl.bookfunnel.com/5zrxylokh0

Yan Tao's daily routine as the proprietor of the Green Brocade Inn is similar to most other proprietors: manage the books, order ingredients, train the staff, greet guests.

And clean up broken furniture.

Green Brocade is better known by its nickname in the world of the *jianghu* — the Broken Furniture Inn. For some reason, the popular stopping place draws in martial artists intent on proving their honor and settling grudges. Yan Tao is tired of heroes wrecking his place and his inn is always another brawl away from bankruptcy. But when a group of bandits appears, the fate of his inn rests in the hands of a young pugilist with a mysterious past.

ALSO BY JF LEE

THE TALES OF THE SWORDSMAN

Vol. 1

Sword of Sorrow, Blade of Joy

Out now. If you're in this book you may have heard Tao Jun talk about his sworn brother, Li Ming. This series tells his story and his path of revenge. Your favorite magistrate makes his first ever appearance here.

Vol. 2

Fangs of the Black Tiger

The second part of the Tales of the Swordsman continues the adventures of Li Ming and Shu Yan. Following the stunning events of *Sword of Sorrow Blade of Joy*, Li Ming must call on the help of old allies like Tao Jun, and Bai Jingyi.

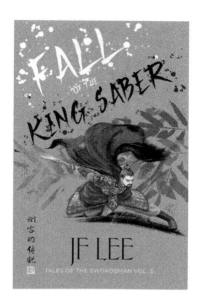

Vol. 3

Fall of the King Saber

Reunited and it feels so good! After a lot of encouragement from our favorite magistrate, Li Ming begins training Shu Yan in the ways of Blue Mountain. But with the Black Tiger Rebellion growing in strength every day, what will happen to the kingdom?

Vol. 4

Sword of the Nine Dragons

Coming soon in 2023. Subscribe to my newsletter for more updates on when this goes live.

ALSO BY JF LEE

THE TALE OF THE MAGISTRATE

THE TOUCH OF MURDER

Sometimes justice punishes the innocent

If it were up to Magistrate Tao Jun, he would solve every mystery with a sword and a fake name (and maybe a fancy silk robe).

So when a missing person becomes a murder investigation, he's (happily) on the case. But all is not as it seems. As the magistrate digs deeper, he finds: an assassin trying to kill him, a trail of blood, a web of lies, and a conman wanted in two cities. And somehow, in the centre of all this deception, is a girl with a mysterious past...

Well, dodging archers' arrows is more fun than paperwork anyway.

Set amid JF Lee's the *Tales of the Swordsman* and the *Tales of the Jianghu* series, this is a detective story with wuxia action (a futou-noir story, if you will). This story follows beloved (and totally corrupt) Magistrate Tao Jun and his dry and irreverent take on the jianghu and the bureaucracy of being a magistrate.

If you like classic wuxia and detective stories, dust off your favorite sword (wipe off those bloodstains—no one needs to see that), and head over to the magistrate's office for **THE TOUCH OF MURDER.**

ALSO BY JF LEE

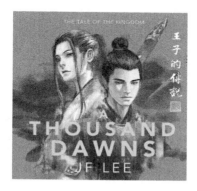

A THOUSAND DAWNS

Prince Zhao Min is happy being a nobody prince. He's not anywhere in the succession plans for the kingdom, and he's happy that way. But when his evil brother seizes the throne for himself, he knows he has to survive long enough to restore peace.

Feng Sun, the beautiful warrior without equal, must keep the prince alive. She swore an oath to help him take the throne, and some promises are meant to be held at all costs.

Even as the kingdom falls, out of the ashes something new arises. Will their hearts stand in the way of what needs to be done for all under heaven? Or will they sacrifice it all for the kingdom?

LOOKING FOR MORE?

Join the Cultivation Novel Group on Facebook for more recommendations and discussion about Wuxia, Xianxia, and Cultivation novels.

ABOUT THE AUTHOR

JF Lee currently resides in the Cayman Islands. He loves a good hat and telling stories about heroes with swords in wuxia settings. He's always thinking about the next adventure to write and where it'll take him. When he's not working on his next novel, he can be found diving for green sea turtles to photograph.

Stay Updated
For the latest in writing and updates, sign up for JF Lee's newsletter at JFLee.co
or join his Facebook group at https://www.facebook.com/JFLeeAuthor/.

Printed in Great Britain
by Amazon

10202458R00113